# TIMIN(  ⎯RICK

## ZOE PARKER

# CONTENTS

*To Echo, who gifted the world with her presence for a brief hour but left an impact of a lifetime.*

The Fate Caller Series

Book Three

# Timing of Trick

## Zoe Parker

# FOREWORD

## A Fairy Song - William Shakespeare

Over hill, over dale,
    Thorough bush, thorough brier,
    Over park, over pale,
    Thorough flood, thorough fire!
    I do wander everywhere,
    Swifter than the moon's sphere;
    And I serve the Fairy Queen,
    To dew her orbs upon the green;
    The cowslips tall her pensioners. Book;
    In their gold coats spots you see;
    Those be rubies, fairy favours;
    In those freckles live their savours;
    I must go seek some dewdrops here,
    And hang a pearl in every cowslip's ear.

**To the reader:**

*This story was a bit harder than the others to write. There are some twists and turns that even I wasn't expecting. It doesn't end on a cliffhanger, I was gentle this time, but it will leave you with questions. Those will be answered in the fourth and final book, Ballad Of Bael. I'm hoping that I can give you the ending this series deserves in the fourth book. This one is a bit short, but I try to price all of my books affordably, and this one is no different. Bear with me. Book four will take the cake.*

*Pre-order coming soon!*

# CHAPTER 1
## THE ELF HAS GONE MENTAL

The man who helped make me is even more psycho than my mom was, and that's saying a lot. I stare down the long, wooden dining table at him, my teeth grit in anger and a little fear, wondering if I can stab him with the steak knife before anyone catches me. He raises his eyebrows, smirking a little as if he knows exactly what I'm thinking.

Not that I'm trying to hide it much. I relax my death grip on the knife and attempt a false smile. It probably looks more like a grimace, but it's all I have left to give.

When I woke up, almost two weeks ago, after he took me from outside of the courthouse, it was in a bedroom made for a child. Pink, so much pink that it gave me vertigo, coats every surface in the room. Then you have the dolls, creepy and also pink, that line one whole side of the room in rows of porcelain horror. There's even a small kitchen playset against the wall opposite the small, pink frilled bed.

Of course, the first thing I did was try to escape, I tore the pink canopy off the bed and tried to make a rope with it to climb out the window. That didn't work out well for me, and I have the bruises to prove it. I was halfway down the outside of the house when Daya cut the homemade rope and let me fall the rest of the way. He then had his acolytes hold me down while he beat me with a switch like the ill-behaved child he called me. That didn't stop me from doing it again the first chance I got. That time they used a bigger switch and chained me to the bed for an entire day.

It took me a full week of trying to fight my way out and various, increasingly more painful punishments for me to settle down for the wait and see approach. After a few days of that, I grew impatient and tried to use my abilities on his staff. It didn't work either. There's a dampener here that pushed back against me and gave me a blinding headache and no results. I have yet to test every room I've been to, but I know it doesn't work in the bedroom, dining room, or their twisted version of a family room.

He has people chained all along the walls in the family room. When I tried to free them, he had the only one I managed to get free, executed.

Treating me like a child doesn't stop with the room either. The clothes they're providing for me to wear are adult-sized but not adult-themed. Childish and a myriad of pastels they're not something you'd put an adult in. The one I'm wearing now is a pukey mint green, covering me from my chin to the tips of my toes in stiff, heavy material. The collar gave me a rash around my neck. I fidget to keep from itching it again; the last time he threatened to tie me to the chair and have one of his servants feed me.

Daya—I refuse to call him dad—instructed me on how to use my napkin, silverware, and not to rest my elbows on the table. He's been droning on for over an hour about mostly himself and his lengthy list of accomplishments as a high priest for Donn. I'm only half listening because he might give me something I need to get out of this mess.

"It's rude to ignore your dinner companion, daughter," he chides, his soft voice echoing in the painfully quiet room.

My head snaps up, and I meet his mismatched eyes. Shit.

He wipes his mouth with his napkin and sits it off to the side. Smiling that creepy smile that makes my skin crawl, he says, "Did you know that I tried to breed a child for over a hundred years? I picked a woman from every race that I thought would be compatible and attempted to plant my seed in their detestable wombs. There were so many failures that, until your mother, I had almost given up hope." He pauses as the staff clears away his plate and gives him a fresh drink of some type, which is tasted by one of the servants for poison first. They do the same with mine even though I only eat when I have to.

"You had other siblings, of course, not that any of them survived the wretched wombs of their mothers. All of them died at birth, until you." *Oh, yay for me.* "I'd have raised you myself if not for that despicable woman. She hid you away from me in her precious forest." Mada? That's the only one I can think of that could be considered living in a forest.

It's good to know that he can't breach that domain.

"Then she had the audacity to let you bond with the scum of Faerie. And those other two losers. There are minions of Donn that are far better suited to be bonded with you." Him speaking about the bonds makes me automatically search for them inside of me.

I find nothing and my heart clenches. Blinking, I fight back the tears of loss. He callously ripped them away from me, and it damn near broke me. I love them, all of them and not feeling them after having them be so intertwined with me is almost enough to defeat me.

Almost.

"I expected you to be more conversational, Keri. Aren't you enjoying the luxury of your new home?"

Watching his face closely, and seeing the veiled threat there, makes me open my mouth and stupidly say, "I'm not going to bond with any of your lackeys." Instantly, I bite the inside of my cheek to stop my out of control mouth before it gets me whipped again, or worse.

"I will control your gift, Keri, one way or another. Even if I have to bond with you myself."

Repulsion churns my stomach, and I clench my hands into fists in my lap to keep my silence. Is he messed up enough to bond with his daughter in that way? Watching the smile play about his mouth and the way his eyes look at me, I get my answer.

Yeah, he would.

"Do you have any idea how valuable a gift you have? You can control the very fate of a person. You alone can defy the laws of Faerie and Donn and bring forth their predetermined fate whenever you want to, and the only repercussion you get for it is a mark. A trivial thing in exchange for such power. It demonstrates how special my seed is to give you such a gift." Ew, just ew. "When Donn told me to go forth and create a child, I didn't understand it at first, but seeing you sitting before me and knowing what you can do—now I understand. You're a gift from my god, and I *will* control you."

One of the biggest things I've noticed about him since I've been here is how he can go from pleasant to deadly in the same sentence without the look on his face changing. I've yet to see anything other than mild annoyance on his face, no matter what I've done. Even when I killed one of his servants, he didn't stop smiling that patient, empty smile that makes me want to run away as fast as I can. I know crazy when I see it, and Daya is the epitome of it.

"Nothing to say?" he asks quietly.

"I won't bond with you or anyone else, Daya. No matter what you do to me, it's not happening." My answer is barely more than a whisper, but sound carries in this room, and he hears it.

His eyes flash black, and that polite mask creaks as his jaw clenches, but then he takes a breath, and the pleasant psycho is back.

"I see that you need more breaking. I want you to know this pains me more than you." He wiggles his hand to one of the servants standing behind me, and when I'm grabbed, I'm not surprised. For a second, I consider fighting, then change my mind. It won't serve any purpose, not today. I pissed him off.

Darkness stirs in my soul, it's always been there, but I tend to push it down and try to ignore it, but I can't—not this time. Smiling, all teeth, I look at him and say, "One day, I'll kill you, Daya. I am my mother's daughter in that way."

As I'm dragged away, I hear him laughing, but it's not as confident as he's pretending, and that makes me smile under the hair covering my face. I'll rip that mask off his face yet.

Ciar

"*Two weeks and we've got nothing, Ciar.*" Trick says, sitting on the couch to run his hand through his messy hair.

Pacing behind him, I spare him a single look before my eyes land on Rime. He's sitting at the opposite end from Trick and playing one of his silly, human video games. There's a smile hovering about this mouth that has me bothered, and I'm not sure why. Out of the three of us, he's been the calmest. Amazingly.

And incredibly out of character.

"Rime, you're not worried?" I ask softly, watching him through my lashes for his reaction.

"Of course I am," he answers without looking away from his game. "I figure you'll come up with something, and there's no point in me confusing the issue."

That's very blasé of him and not how someone should be if their Center is missing. Our bonds were torn away and left Trick and myself reeling. The day it happened, he was as upset as we were. That's not the case anymore.

Is this perhaps how he copes with traumatic things? No, he's lived many lives before this, and no matter how immature he acts at times, he'd be able to cope with trauma.

Trick is looking at him now too with suspicion marring his brow. The bond connecting the three of us is incredibly faint and fading as time slips by, but it does still exist. I use it and my other senses to look at him. He looks the same, smells the same, and there's no aura of magic around him. Overall, I can't see any reason to think he's not anything more than an asshole.

Trick's gaze meets mine, and I shrug. He's always been different than either of us, but because her bond called to him, I accepted it. No, I tolerate it—for Keri's sake.

On reflex, I reach out for her, hoping to feel the fiery essence of her and get nothing. Sitting on the bottom step of the staircase I stare out the window in the front door. I've spent almost every day with her for years, half of them in love with her, and not having her part of me—part of my day—is awful.

*Faerie, please... please help me get her back.*

This isn't the first time I've prayed to the goddess for help, but it is the first time that tears burn my eyes and my heart feels like it's in my throat. Keri isn't just my Center. She's my life, and not being able to find her—let alone save her—is the most frustrating, painful moment in my life.

The pull on my soul shocks me enough that I gasp. When vertigo fades, I'm floating in brightly lit, color-filled space, surrounded by the essence of Faerie herself.

*My son, what causes you such pain?*

Clearing my throat, I answer her plainly, *The High-Priest of Donn has taken my mate.*

*I have this knowledge, but why does it hurt you so?*

Angry I lash out, *I love her more than life itself! You gave her to me only to take her away!*

The world around me shifts, and darkness leeches the color out of the air. I've made her angry, and for the first time, I don't care.

*It is not for you to decide her fate, or question the plan for her.*

*Then whose decision is it? Yours? A god who only meddles in the fate of mortals to entertain yourself?*

In all my years, I've never spoken to Faerie in such a way, and even with the knowledge that she can take my life, I feel no different. Keri means more to me than anything, even the one who created me.

*You love her greatly, Lord of the Hunt.*

*Yes, yes, I do.*

*Do you know why I created you, Ciar?*

As always, she speaks of something other than what I ask but given no other choice, I answer her. *To lead the hunt of justice... and to be some king of an unknown crown.*

*Yes, but there is more. When the idea of you came to me, I gave you something none of my other children possess. I carried you in my womb... gave you part of my essence. You are the only one of your kind because it weakened me to bring you into existence. You matter more than any other creature to me, Ciar, and I admit, I do not like to see you so unhappy.*

All of this is news to me, but I don't know what to do with it. Nor do I know what it has to do with Keri. *If you dislike my unhappiness, please give me a way to get her back.*

7

*Your duty to the Fae and the Hunt matter more than your connection to a woman.*

*Maybe to you, but not to me. I will refuse the Hunt, and I will reject the crown—if I have to I will scorch the worlds in search of her and go to war with Donn and his disciples.*

*You will lose against one such as he, Ciar.*

*That doesn't matter—at least I will have tried!*

*Even if it means your destruction?*

*Yes, even then.*

My life would be empty without her and not worth living. If it's the cost of trying to get her back and save her from the psychopath that has her in his clutches, my life will gladly be forfeit.

*Will you finally seek out the crown if I give you a boon? Will you accept your true fate and the trials it requires?*

*Yes, anything.*

Faerie chuckles, and the hair on my arms rises. *I made a wise choice, choosing her for you. Just as I did creating you. Go forth, son of Faerie, and try to save your mate... but be warned you are not bound to a weak soul. Learn to have faith in her as she does you. This flower must be planted where the wards meet the earth. You will be able to get word to her but not bring her out. That is something that she must do for herself, Ciar.*

The colors return, smothering the darkness, and a single white flower floats towards me. Reaching out, I grab it and pull it close to my chest to protect it. I had already decided to seek the crown, to protect Keri and our Triad, but I was procrastinating about it.

*Thank you, Faerie.*

When I blink, I'm back on the stairs in the foyer of the house. Trick is looking at me in surprise, and Rime is still focused on his game.

"I may have a way to get to Keri," I say into the silence. Trick stands and crosses to me.

"What do we do?" he asks.

Smiling, I hold up the flower. "Faerie granted me a boon. We have a way to contact her now."

Trick

AFTER CIAR AND I SPOKE AND AGREED UPON OUR COURSE of action, I went in search of the items we need, and as I walked down the stairs, the sight at the door stopped me dead in my tracks. Something wearing Keri's face has its tongue down Rime's throat. I know it's not her. I felt her presence even without the bond, and this creature is a void and makes me feel nothing but repulsion. How the fuck doesn't he see beyond the false face? Has the snowman lost his mind now that the bond is in pieces?

I know it's not Keri, but Rime doesn't seem to care. Leaping down the stairs, I grab him and shove him away. My hand transforms into a sword, and I run it through the heart of the creature that stares at me in surprise... with Keri's eyes. My heart twists even though I know it's not her.

The skin of the dying creature shrinks and collapses in on itself as it starts to dissolve. I pull back away from it and watch it turn into a pile of goop on the floor. I turn to Rime angrily.

"That wasn't Keri, you idiot! Have you gone daft? Didn't you feel the wrongness of it?" I demand.

He glares at me and says, "How was I supposed to know? She was all over me the minute I opened the door!"

"Because you should feel her, you idiot! Think of her with more than your dick." His fist flying at my face is easy to

9

avoid. Rime is strong, but out of the three, he's also the weakest. Something I don't think he realizes yet.

He keeps swinging at me, and I keep dodging, reluctant to hit him. When Keri returns—because she *will* fucking return —she might get mad at me for hurting him. He's a twat, but he's still part of our Triad, and fighting with him will solve nothing.

I'm starting to think that the bond breaking has broken his mind as well. He's not acting right and hasn't been since she was taken from outside of the courthouse.

"What are you doing, Rime? The last thing in the world Keri would want is for you to be fighting each other," Zag says, flapping down the staircase to grab a claw full of Rime's hair. Effortlessly, the miniature dragon drags him backward and out of reach. He might be small, but some things don't change, no matter how much you shrink.

"I don't give a shit what she wants. She left me," Rime yells, fast walking out of the open door, leaving nothing but a touch of frost in his wake.

"He's not right, Zag," I muse, watching him disappear down the sidewalk.

"Separation like this can be detrimental to a fragile mind; the bond goes deep, and its forced removal can break someone," Zag says, landing on the railing. "Although, he's never quite acted right since he came here, he's powerful, and his soul is old, even if his body isn't. Although, I do agree that something is off about him. He seems angry at Keri versus being angry at the man who took her."

"I have my sympathies for the twat, but we need him focused on getting our girl back. Not feeling sorry for himself."

"I agree. In this case, though, there isn't a choice. I fear he's worthless to be currently counted upon for aid, so we'll have to make do without him. What is the plan so far?" Zag flaps over to land on the railing, his eyes still on the open door.

"Faerie gave Ciar a way to breach the wards so we can talk to her. Can't fucking rescue her, but we can have a spot of tea and conversation." The gods and their ilk have never done anything good for me, and I don't put much water into their gifts.

"At least you'll be able to talk to her. That's more than you have now."

The damn scaly bastard had to go and be the voice of reason. I want to be mad, not logical. With a sigh, I wipe a hand down my face. "We have to find her first. We have a general idea but nothing concrete. I'm going to sneak in and see what I can find out."

"Exactly what all can you turn into?" Zag asks curiously.

Smiling, I raise an eyebrow. "Anything."

"Did I miss something exciting?" Ciar asks dryly, walking up the front steps to stand on the porch. His eyes glance at the melting frost on the floor and walls.

Turning to him, I answer, "Rime was making out with a Keri doppelganger and got pissy when I pointed it out and killed it."

"I ran into one in town as well. How did he not feel the wrongness of it?" Ciar asks, stepping inside the house and closing the door.

"I don't know, he seems... off."

"That's putting it mildly. We're pretty sure he's had an emotional break of some type, and it's sent him spiraling off into insanity," Zag says, blowing shadows at me.

"What he said," I answer, hooking a thumb towards Zag.

"Perhaps we should follow him and check on his welfare. The last thing in the world I want to explain to Keri is that we allowed something to eat him." Laughing at Ciar's words, I follow him out the door, I don't even care when Zag lands on my shoulder—something he's never done before. I realize how much the dragon misses her too.

It's not hard to catch up with Ciar, he's walking fast, but my legs are as long as his. He stops at the cross street and sniffs the air, and then we head straight for the butcher shop where Keri works. Lo and behold Rime is once again in the arms of another doppelganger. One who is trying to sneakily draw out his life force.

He has completely lost his flipping mind.

"At least now we know why they're targeting us. They're leeches of some type. The fact that they can get so close to him so quickly is concerning. I think we need to find out more about our feeble-minded friend, Trick. This behavior doesn't make sense," Ciar says, stopping me with a hand on my elbow. I look over my shoulder at him, and he's looking at the fake Keri clenching his jaw.

"I know a place I can find out information, but there will be a cost," Zag muses, a tuft of smoke coming out of his nostrils and wafting directly into my face. I blow it away and give him a look out of the corner of my eye.

"Whatever it is, we'll pay it," I reassure him.

"It is not you who will make the payment. I'll return as soon as I have something," Zag says, lifting into the sky and growing as he climbs higher.

"Well, let's be on about it and get rid of this parasite," Ciar says, moving so fast that he's already beside Rime. That's a neat trick, lucky bastard.

Grabbing the fake Keri by the head, he flicks his hand, and her neck snaps with a loud crack. Rime cries out and falls to the ground with her. Kneeling, he watches the body entirely dissolve before turning to look up at Ciar, his face full of grief. I join them and cross my arms.

"Rime, what the fuck?" Ciar demands.

"I can't help myself... when I see her face, I lose all control and must go to her." The words seem almost forced out of him, and for the first time, I truly realize the depth of whatever is wrong with him.

I've seen that type of madness before.

"But you have to know it's not the real her," I demand, pointing at the bubbling circle of goo.

"I'm not sure what I know anymore. It's the stupid curse," he mutters, barely loud enough for me to hear and climbs to his feet. Full out running—running away is his new reaction to everything—he disappears around a corner and is gone. This time Ciar makes no move to follow him.

"Curse? The lad shouldn't have a curse and be able to bond with Keri," Ciar muses, turning on his heel and heading back towards the house.

I stare at the puddle a few moments longer before I follow in his wake. I don't know much about the Triad bond, I mostly followed my instincts to come to her, and the bits and pieces mum spoke of years back has helped me along too. That's my limit on knowledge. In this, I'll trust Ciar all the way.

And if Rime has a curse and isn't supposed to be able to bond with Keri, that's a big concern for her and us. Curse or no, Keri is the glue that holds us together in every way. That's the bad side of a Triad and their Center. There is no life without them.

We have to get our girl back, and that might be Rime's only hope—if there is any to be had.

## CHAPTER 2
## ONE LEFT SHOE

I might not have a lot of magic—besides the fate stuff—but I'm good at finding it. Bored, I went through the entire room and found several Snoop spells and the odd Peek-aboo ones. They weren't hard to get rid of, which I did, and now I'm annoyed that someone has been listening and watching me this entire time. Not that I've been doing more than mumbling death threats under my breath, but that's not the point.

It's unsettling.

Everything about this place is like that. It got so bad while I was looking around that I turned all of the dolls backward because I'm sick of them staring at me and making me feel like they're *actually* watching me. I checked them for spells; there aren't any, but why he set up this awful room is beyond me. We both know he has no sentiment concerning me, and this room is a mockery of any parental feelings if nothing else.

He really is a psychopath.

Disgusted with my situation, I drop on the end of the bed and cross my arms. Staring out the window, I wonder if I can survive falling three stories. The worst thing that can happen is I break a leg—or two. Then I can't run and have to face the wrath of Daya. Death should be the worst, but in this case, I don't think it is.

With a sigh, I give up the brief thought of jumping.

When something thumps against the window, I frown. When it happens again, I cross to the window and open it. On the ground below my window is a large stick. There aren't any trees close by, so my eyes automatically lift to scan the edge of the property. Waving arms in the distance makes my heart beat fast.

Ciar is standing there, waving his arm at me, in his hand, is a bright blue shoe. Even at this distance, I can see his smile as he throws the shoe towards me. Reflexively I duck out of the way, and the shoe thumps to the floor. Turning to it, I watch in amazement as the shoe begins to twitch, and in the next breath, Trick is standing there smiling at me. I run into his arms and press myself against him so hard it's nearly painful. Burying my face in his shirt, I breathe in the smell of him—wildness and mint.

Gently, he pushes me away from him to look down at me. "I don't have long before they notice the intrusion, but we wanted to check on you and let you know we're working on finding a way to get you out of here," he says hurriedly.

"You're not here to rescue me?" The hope that was blooming in my chest dies a horrible death as he grimaces.

"Not this time. We don't know how to get you out of here without him knowing. The gift we were given only allows us to make brief contact, and talking Ciar out of storming in here wasn't easy. Even after he said he shouldn't be the one to come in."

"I don't understand."

"The wards are keyed to you, if we try to take you out of

them without taking them down first, it'll kill you. That sneaky fucker thought of everything."

"Except you sneaking in here as a shoe, apparently," I tease although my heart isn't in it. When I saw Ciar and then Trick, I was so sure they were here to save me. But I'll take what I can get. His presence is a balm on the painful chaos being here has wrought.

"We'll come up with something, I swear it." He kisses me, short and sweet, but intense enough to make my lips tingle. "There are doppelgangers of you all over the place. I'm not sure of their purpose, but they're becoming a nuisance."

I know why they exist, and it pisses me off. "Decoys for spells and probably to mess with you guys. How's Ciar, Zag? Fluffy and Rime?" He grimaces again at my question, and for the first time, I get worried. "Spill it."

"If only I had the time to explain. Rime isn't right, and there are some things about him being bonded to you that aren't making sense."

"What do you mean?"

"He has a curse, Keri. From what Ciar said, a curse should prevent him from bonding with you." This isn't good, not at all. He's right; a curse is essentially a bond of a different type linked to whoever placed it. That should stop any other bonds from forming an anchor to another, at least naturally. That leaves only one option: if he's cursed, then he hijacked the bond.

Pain tightens my chest. I've shared my body and heart with the man and to find out that he's potentially not the one I'm supposed to be bonded to cracks my heart, but I shove it down. I focus on the more critical part of it. There are nefarious reasons he took the bond because someone who fights being held down that hard don't choose something like that. They run from it.

Unfortunately, it's something I'll have to deal with later.

There are more important things to worry about now, like escaping this place.

"We will get you out of here."

"When exactly will that happen?" The clock is ticking, and Daya will start doing more dangerous things to get what he wants. I don't tell Trick this, it'll just worry them, but I know time is running out and how badly Daya reacts to failure.

"I'm not sure, but I promise we'll come up with something soon. You have one of the strongest Fae in existence determined to get you out, and Ciar doesn't lose."

Neither does Daya, who's protected from Ciar, but I don't say that. I have to have faith in him in them. Maybe I need to have more confidence in myself.

"Who gave you this... whatever it is, to get in here?" I ask.

"Faerie... but Ciar had to agree to her quest bullshit. Which we all have to be there for."

Always a catch with a god, always. "Why not just magic way to get me out? I don't get it." But I kind of do. Faerie is always about testing and growth and all of the bullshit that goes along with it. She never flat out helps you; it's about you becoming more through conflict. Why can't anything ever be simple with magic or gods?

"You know how Faerie is, there's always fucking complications," he answers, giving me another quick kiss. His phone starts beeping, attracting his attention—he looks down at it and grits his teeth, before dropping a quick kiss on my lips. "Leaving you here is going against everything I believe in, but I'll be back. Stay safe, Keri." In a run, he heads towards the window and leaps smoothly out of it, and when I cross the room, a deer is running swiftly towards Ciar.

Ciar's green eyes light up, and I know he's trying to talk to me in my mind, but whatever magic Daya has on the house is blocking it all. The moment he realizes it, his eyes cloud with anger then immediately clear. With a saucy wink, he turns, and the guys disappear into the forest. I don't need words to know how he feels about me. His eyes said it all.

Shutting the window, I go back to the bed and sit cross-legged with my back resting against the headboard.

Now I can think about the worst part of this whole experience so far. Trick essentially said my snowflake might not be mine. Sharp pain in my chest forces me to rub just above my heart. The thoughts crawl through my brain like glass, needing to be dealt with before they take me to a dark place I can't crawl back out of in order to help my damn self.

Can it be true? Is the man that I've grown to love, in a sense, an imposter? I picture his smile and bright blue eyes, and a tear slides down my face. Is he so good at being duplicitous that I was snowballed that easily? He was so reluctant in the beginning, playing hard to get... so damn genuine. Was it all a lie?

Is that why I'm so confused when it comes to Bael because *he* was meant for it instead?

This hurts more than anything Daya can do to me. I love Rime and if he's betrayed me somehow... I don't know what I'll do about that. I don't know what *Ciar* will do about it; not because he loves Rime—I'm not even sure he likes Rime—but because he loves me. With a sob held back in my throat, I swipe a hand down my face and force the tears away. I can't let it be the end of it yet, not until I talk to him, hear his point of view.

But I won't be bonding with him again either. The guys are right; someone with a curse can't bond in a Triad. Rime's a liar, but I can't condemn him until I know exactly how much he's lied about. That doesn't stop the hardening of my heart. I don't have any choice.

He isn't mine and never was.

For several hours I sit numbly, looking out the window

focused only on how to get out of here. Matters of the heart aren't as high a priority as getting away from Daya before he either succeeds at enslaving me or beats me to death. The guys are strong, unique in their own ways—well, two of them now—but sitting here waiting for rescue isn't going to get me rescued. I need to figure out a way to do it myself.

*Come on, brain, give me something to work with.*

Three days later...

I'VE WRACKED MY BRAIN, NONSTOP, AND I STILL HAVEN'T thought of a way to get out of here. My magic doesn't want to work right, and I've yet to find out what's specifically blocking my 'specialized' magic. With a situation like this, the individuals have to be protected with a bespelled item. Wards can stop one thing, sometimes two, but they can't blanket every person residing in the protected area. Whatever it is, it can be broken like any other spell. I just have to find the item it's attached to.

Now that we're on our way to another 'family' dinner, I take this opportunity to search for it. We're almost to the dining room when I realize what it is. Each one of the guards is wearing a stone around their necks. Its gold in color and, if you stare at it long enough, pulses a little like a heartbeat.

That also means that Daya is wearing one like it somewhere on his person too. That can pose a problem. Daya is strong—perhaps even as strong as Ciar—and he has magic that can seriously hurt me. But, I look around the room at the silent guards lining the walls and doorways, Daya isn't always around.

He disappears all the time, sometimes for the whole day, doing whatever High Priests of Donn do. That might present a chance for me to rescue myself. When he looks down to cut into his steak with a smirk of arrogance on his face, I palm the steak knife and slide it into my sleeve. When no one reacts or says anything, I put my hands in my lap and tuck the knife into the pocket of the ridiculous pink smock he made me wear.

The guards aren't the most observant lot, but that kind of makes sense, considering I don't think any of them have thoughts of their own. I'm pretty sure they're thralls, which means their souls were sacrificed and their bodies enslaved by Daya. Puppets. Calling their fates to them, in all of their cases, will be a mercy.

I don't consider their deaths my fault.

That thought gives me the solid resolve to do everything I can get to the fuck out of here. And as soon as Daya is gone, I plan to enact that resolve. I'm tired of being the 'princess in the tower' guarded by the dragon, waiting on prince charming to save me.

I'm going to be my own damn hero and ride the fucking dragon into the sunset.

## CHAPTER 3
## A CURSE A DAY...

Trick

The book that Zag brought back has a lot of information, even about things I didn't know existed. The dragon looks tired and is missing several scales. I'm guessing that was part of the cost. Those mystic bitches who tend to keep shit like this always ask for something that either involves pain or humiliation. Sadistic twats, the whole lot of them. As if handing someone a book is a hard thing to do.

My mum was no different than the rest of them. She conceived me with a sacrifice spell and tried to twist me into *her* creature. She almost succeeded too. But her sister—my aunt—told me that my destiny lay elsewhere and freed me from my shackles. The emotional and physical ones. It cost her greatly. When my mum tried to stop us, my aunt sacrificed herself to save me. My freedom was gained by both of their deaths, and although it pained me, killing my mum was the only way for me to survive.

*Off those morbid thoughts, boyo.*

I take a deep breath and focus on what Zag is saying. Keri is what's important now, not my shite baggage.

"Jack Frost, as he is named here… is a soul that lives a mortal life until he dies. And then after a period of imbalance is reborn once again. However," Zag pauses and turns a page with one claw, "in his second incarnation, the fool, seduced a Fairy princess and left her at the altar, heartbroken. Unfortunately for him, she knew what he was. Broken-hearted, she cursed him never to be able to love and retain his sanity at the same time."

That's fucked.

"Then how did he bond with Keri?" Ciar demands way more calmly than I can pull off, it's why I'm keeping my mouth shut.

"As we already suspected, he had to have stolen the bond from its true target. I'm guessing that someone helped him, someone powerful. Otherwise, he wouldn't have been able to complete it," Zag answers, showing a bit of tooth. Like Ciar and I, he sees the implications of this and how fucked up they are.

"The usual suspects, I presume?" Ciar sits beside Zag on the bed and reads through the pages that Zag was reading aloud. "We all know that someone stealing a bond with a Center isn't unheard of, it happens quite frequently but usually by someone who is also compatible. This is not the case in our situation. We were all fooled." Something that doesn't make him very happy, nor me. Both of us didn't question his presence because Keri didn't question it. We should have looked closer, but neither one of us smelled anything foul about it.

It does explain Keri's slightly less heated response to him versus Ciar, and even myself—if I do say so. Perhaps her magic *was* telling her something was off?

"Do you think he's faked having feelings for her?" If that's the case, I'm going to kick his ass—twice. The look on her face when I told her about him was pure hurt. She hid it fast but seeing it made my stomach ache. The woman loves him as she does Ciar and, maybe even me.

"The bond would've enhanced things, but it can't make you feel something for someone that isn't already blossoming. I think as much as he's able to, he does love her—which explains the insanity—but the fact of the matter is, he couldn't have bonded to her without help, and I'm leaning towards Daya." Ciar taps his finger on his chin, a habit I've seen before. The claw peeking out of the tip of his finger is new and shows how unsettled he truly is.

Zag breaks in with, "I think it was meant for our lovely neighbor, Bael. He's the one that's drawn to her as you two were. The intensity of it can't be faked, and there's a disgusting amount of intensity there. You can see it in how he looks at her."

"I thought he simply desired something out of reach," Ciar muses. We all know how Ciar feels about the Duke and his father, but he didn't threaten Bael away. This means he suspected Bael belonged with Keri from the beginning—he just didn't like the fact.

"We've all been had, gents. And poor Keri will be the one who suffers the most for it," I say into the suddenly silent room. "We all know that when Daya took her, he did something to our bond, and that's when Rime started this foolish behavior. Is it possible that when the bond was broken, or in the least severely damaged, it also broke the spell that helped him steal the bond to begin with?"

"With strong enough magic, it would've completely masked the other bond. Although," he turns to Zag, "it also leaves him bare to the genuine feelings he has for her. I also have to agree about Bael. She saw something with him, I saw it too, and the way he looks at her is how we look at her."

"How do we fix this for Keri?" I demand. Because really that's what it's about. He bonded with her. However he did it, and even though the bond is broken, he needs to be cut off from ever receiving it again. His feelings, genuine or not, don't matter when his magical relationship with her is bullshit.

I think that Ciar and I are in the same boat about it. I still feel the same for her, and nothing has changed, bond or not. I'm hers and will forever be.

"We tell her the truth and let her make her own choices. Ultimately she'll do the right thing for her, whether we agree with it or not," Zag reassures me, confident in her abilities.

Which brings up the slight error I might have had in judgment. "I might have done told her something about it."

Ciar's eyes narrow. "You told her that while she's confined in that place?"

"She has a right to know, us not telling her things is what causes problems to begin with." I'm right, and he knows it, it's why he doesn't argue, but he's also right. It's something that might have been left until she is free of that hell hole. Bad timing on my part for transparency.

"Is there a chance that it has to do with his curse and not some nefarious reason? That perhaps he is strong enough to bond despite it?" Ciar asks the miniature dragon. Whether it's to hope to save Keri heartache or to stop her from one day bonding with Bael, I don't know, but they're solid questions to ask. So I say nothing.

"I don't know. Rime is an enigma when it comes to his true intentions. However, we can agree that he did steal the bond. Being cursed would've prevented her magic from seeking him out and even freely allowing him to bond at all. Whether on purpose or not, it's happened." Zag rests on the bed like a big cat and flicks his tail in irritation. "We can't confront him until we get Keri out of there. There's always a chance it's connected to Daya, and we could put her in even more danger interfering too soon."

I nod, agreeing with him. The last thing in the world we want to do is make things harder for Keri. None of us have any idea what her father is putting her through. Just the thought makes me clench my teeth so hard they creak. I've only ever felt this helpless once in my life, and that didn't end well.

"We act normal and keep him in the dark about our plans concerning Keri," Ciar says, standing and crossing to the window that looks into Bael's house. "Do we bring in the Duke?"

"Do you think he's trustworthy?" I ask.

"When it comes to Keri, yes. That also means anything connected to Keri is safe from his machinations. Anything else, probably not."

"Isn't she what matters the most?" I demand, wishing he'd drop his prejudice and move forward with what needs to be done.

"Yes, and that's why we'll bring him in. I'm a fool for being complacent about a bond that didn't feel right to me and probably even more so for championing a bond with the son of a man I detest. I mistakenly thought that because of how rare he was... as you and I are, that Rime was the right fit. Even though my instincts said differently, Bael, on the other hand, is at least double his strength, and so many other things are now glaringly obvious... I won't repeat that mistake even if I'm not happy with the choices."

Looking at him, as shadows gather closer to him and the

feeling of *other* saturates the room, I completely understand why he's the Lord of the Hunt and freely admit, only to myself, that he intimidates me more than I'm comfortable with.

"So, what's the plan?" I prompt, expecting him to say more than he did. He looks at me and after a moment of contemplation, shrugs.

"In my current... position, I can't harm Daya, and his wards are incredibly strong. Even a gift from Faerie herself struggled to hold them open long enough for us to send you through. If I go to war with them, using the Sluagh as soldiers, I won't win, and we'll all die for nothing."

"Why didn't you go in and see her too." Not that I'm complaining about him sending me in. I got to see her at least. "I get the whole angry thing, I'm right there with you, but she could've used your comfort the most."

"The temptation to lay havoc to that household would've been too strong for me to resist and would put her in even more danger. Because ultimately, I can't touch Daya, and he will use her to hurt us and vice versa," Ciar explains, unmoving from the window. "There's a doppelganger in Bael's bedroom, and he's just woken up and saw her."

Jumping to my feet, I cross the room to watch the drama unfold. This is a test on whether or not Bael deserves to be part of Keri's life. If he recognizes the fake in front of him, then the bond is calling him. I'm not entirely sure how I feel about it on a personal level, but I don't have the same prejudices against the Fae Duke that Ciar has. Mine is more about whether he'll hurt her like the situation with Rime is bound to.

Bael climbs slowly to his feet, keeping the bed in between him and the lookalike. He's as naked as the day he was born and without any weapons. The doppelganger's presence in Bael's house isn't a surprise. More than likely, they're trying to distract or kill, and from the way she is eyeing Bael, have a little fun in the process.

Bael stands stock still while the fake Keri inches around the bed with a sensual smile on her face. When she gets within a foot, his hands shoot out and latch around the neck. Magic seeps from between his fingers as the creature disintegrates into dust.

Bael saw it for what it is, proving that he—in the least—has more sense than Rime. He's also crazy powerful, and that's something I knew but didn't realize the extent of. I think I was sticking him in the pampered prince box. A spoiled rich man who lives in his father's shadows. In seems in some ways, I was way off the mark.

Dusting his hands, he grabs a pair of pants off the floor and pulls them on. Crossing to the window, he opens it and demands, "Where the fuck is the real Keri?"

Oh, that's right, we didn't tell him.

Ciar opens the window. "How did you know?" he asks Bael softly.

"It didn't feel like her," Bael answers after studying Ciar's face for several moments.

"You should come over, there are things to discuss," Ciar says, shutting the window and heading downstairs. Bael stares at Ciar for a beat and does the same thing. This conversation will be entertaining. I might even get a spot of amusement out of it. Those two see each other as adversaries and will need to come to a reckoning about their places in Keri's life.

When it comes down to it, I'm not here for the measuring of dicks. I'm here for Keri. As long as the ones chosen for her are good to her and not some cursed idiot who more than likely betrayed her, I don't care.

Besides, I can make mine as big as I like.

With a smile tipping my lips, I turn to Zag. "You coming, Dragon?" I ask the dozing lizard.

"I'll be along shortly. I'm sure that you gentlemen will have everything in hand."

That translates to, *I have something I'm going to do, but I don't want you to know.*

And Keri thinks *I'm* mysterious.

## CHAPTER 4
## A BRIDE IN DENIAL

A sense of foreboding shadows the fancy dinner invitation I woke up to, not that any of them are fun. When I opened my eyes, it sat like a crown jewel on the empty pillow next to my head. The paper is soft and feels like fabric as I run my fingers over the flowy golden script. Why he bothered with a written invitation when I'm a prisoner in his house, I'll never know. I'm putting it off on him being crazy. I grew up with it, and he wears the same kind of mask.

Smiles and psychopathy.

Knowing that I don't have a choice, I crumple the invitation and toss it across the room. The last time I refused one of his formal requests, he had them strip me down to my underwear and put my food in a dog bowl. I didn't eat it, but that didn't make the act any less humiliating. With a small sigh of defeat I put on the beautiful green dress that's laid out across the foot of the bed. For once, it's something designed for an adult, and from the look of it, Fairy made.

The sparkling high heels I leave off, the dress is long enough and will hide my bare feet. I've never been fond of that type of shoe, and I can't imagine running in them. Anyone who can is a god in their own right.

The knife I tuck in the top of my bodice; it'll be a pain to get to, but I like the comforting presence of it. If nothing else, it hardens my resolve.

When the dinner gong sounds, I cross to the door and wait for them to open it. The temptation to stab the first guard to poke his head through is intense, but I decide against it. Without actually touching me they use their presence to herd me down the long hallway to the curved staircase and down into the crowded dining room.

Oh, this isn't good.

All of the guests are male. Daya is trying to sell me off like a prize cow. This group reeks of power and prestige, and his intentions are clear as day. He's trying to pick me out a new Triad—there's no way he'd let me pick out my own—not that I would anyhow. Technically, I'm no longer bonded to one but deep inside, hidden—maybe even protected—is a little tiny piece of my family. It's so small that sometimes I don't feel it there at all, but at moments like this, when the world is falling on my head... it's shining in the gloom, reminding me of what's waiting for me outside of this place.

"Daughter," Daya greets, coming around the table to clasp my hands in his cold, soft ones. The urge to pull my hands from him and wipe them on my dress is strong, but I manage to keep mine limp in his grasp. The last time I pulled away from his 'affections,' he had me beat. I'd rather not repeat that tonight, my back still hasn't completely healed.

The minute his grip loosens, I do pull my hands away—his touch is revolting—but I don't give in to the urge to clean them. He'll see me, and that won't go well.

"My esteemed guests, this is my miraculous and only child, Keri." There's a sparkle of happiness in his eyes and an almost genuine smile on his face as he steers me with an unbreakable grip on my arm, from person to person. He introduces me by giving a glowing list of skills and eloquence that I don't possess, but I keep my mouth shut. They're all servants of Donn in one way or another, and most of them don't even bother keeping the leer off their faces while we're speaking to them. In their eyes I'm a valuable commodity, not only for what I can do but also because of who I am. They're not allies of anyone but their god, money, and of course, their High-Priest.

To them, I've become a shiny damn princess, who's nothing more than a trophy to gain. I hate this world.

After the parade of faces and too many heavily applied colognes and cosmetics, I'm thankful when we sit down. Tonight is not the night for me to try and escape. Not only are there dozens of more people here, but they also brought their guards and servants. None of them trust each other; people like this don't. That's too many eyes and enemies together in one room for me to try and escape. If there was someone sympathetic to my plight, things would be easier. An inside person is the key, at least in books. I've never personally had to do it before, and that's what makes me doubt myself.

"Do you see anyone you might wish to be paired with, Keri?" Daya asks, spearing a piece of steak and delicately placing it in his mouth. He chews it with a slow deliberateness that gives me chills. The way he looks at me, appreciative and coveting, is not the way a father looks at his child. Not at all.

He also doesn't care if I like any of them; it's not my choice. So him asking the question is purely for appearance's sake.

I have to get the hell out of here, and that requires me to first get out from underneath the regard of so many assholes. There's one sure way to get sent back to my room.

"No, and there won't be, Daya," I say blithely while watching him perch his fork on the edge of his gold-trimmed plate. Slowly, he wipes his fingers with a napkin and turns to me with the intense scrutiny, one would give a piece of gold that's still precious, but with a flaw that detracts from its value.

"You will refer to me as father, or you will be punished." As usual, his threat is delivered with a smile. I have dreams about punching that smile off his face with a big rock.

"No, you may have created me, but you'll never earn that title," I bite out, standing. "This is a farce, and you know it. I'm not a pet to be paraded around on a golden leash. I won't bond with anyone you bring before me, ever!" I raise my voice, and when it echoes in the silent room, I smirk at Daya, adding something that I know will piss him off. "You are no one to me, and you never will be."

The force of his magic hitting me takes me to the ground, pinning me to the floor. As the cold magic pushes against my skin, crushing the breath from me, I cry out. He's strong and way out of my league power wise, but something about his magic is wrong as if it isn't supposed to exist. My magic reacts to it and makes its contact all the more painful.

His hands force my mouth open, and the foul taste of his blood trickles in, coating my mouth. Using my tongue, I push at the foul-tasting liquid, spitting out as much of it as I can.

The crazy asshole is trying to force me to bond with him!

Thankfully, my magic doesn't like it and is already resisting and destroying his invasive magical blood—burning it, and my skin. I welcome the pain because I will not be bonded to this creature! Magic surges and then fades away when he curses above me. I open my eyes and smile up at him through my burned lips.

"No bond, ever," I bite out.

When he brings his face close enough to me, I use every

bit of strength I have and headbutt him in the mouth. It's dissatisfying that he doesn't even flinch as blood runs from his split mouth and a busted nose. The bright red rivulets slither down his chin and drip onto my dress, ruining the beauty of it. He smiles, and the coldness of it makes my instincts scream at me to run as fast as I can get away from him.

There's a chance I pushed him too far this time.

"You will submit to me, Keri. No matter what it takes, I will force your hand," he threatens in a voice barely above a whisper. There's an edge of excitement to it that makes me think the gross dickhead is getting off on hurting me. That's so ew, just ew. So much so that I gag from the thought of what it entails.

If I throw up in his face, he deserves it and more.

He moves away from me, as if sensing my intentions, and rough hands pull me to my feet. I look around the shocked faces in the room and smile. "I will kill anyone who tries to bond with me," I threaten, meaning every word of it. I refuse to allow such a beautiful thing to be perverted by him or people like him. "Including you, *Daya*."

"Take her to her room, no dinner tonight," Daya orders, wiping at his bloody face with that eerie smile still as wide as ever.

As they lift me to my feet and drag me from the room, I take the opportunity to fall against one, leaning against his chest as I sneak my hand in between us and pull on the necklace experimentally. He doesn't react, and the eyes looking down at me are as dead as a fish's. Carefully watching his blank face, I pull until the leather thong gives, and the necklace slithers into my palm.

Halfway down the hall, well away from the dining room, I repeat the same maneuver with the second guard and get his necklace too. They really are zombies. There's no reactions, no arguments. They're following the specific instructions to take me to my room, and not paying attention to anything that doesn't involve me trying to escape.

It's entirely possible they're not even alive. Donn is the god of the dead, and Daya is his priest. Already my Fate magic stirs, eager to call the fate of them both, but I tamp it down. The only future I can think they're due for is decay, that's what dead things do. I only hope I'm long gone by the time they start to smell—stinking corpses lying around will get noticed.

I'm pushed through the door into my room, and it shuts with a solid thump behind me. Annoyed, I strip off the ruined dress; it's covered in Daya's blood, and despite how pretty it was, I can't associate anything good with it. Looking at it pooled in a crumpled heap on the floor I give into the impulse and take the knife and cut out a square that's saturated in his blood and tuck it away in my bra. It's gross, but blood is a powerful thing, and now I have his.

Crossing to the closet, I dig around and try to find something that isn't lacey or frilly and eventually find a riding outfit in the back. Thank Faerie for some clothing traditions. There are even boots. A muffled curse freezes me in place.

Someone is hiding in there.

Pulling all of the clothes out and tossing them on the floor, I end up uncovering a small person huddling under a fallen petticoat. There's only one creature I know that skulks around in closets, a Brownie.

"Hello," I greet in an even, friendly tone. I don't want to scare him away, he *is* hiding in my closet, and I imagine it's from Daya and his ilk.

A little pointy brown hat peeks over the edge of the petticoat, followed by matching brown eyes. He peeps out, "Greetings."

"Why are you in the closet?" He lets the petticoat drop

from his face, and I watch his hands knead the material nervously. He's a timid thing, and considering where he lives; I can understand it. Living with Daya is hell on his adult-child, I can't imagine how hard it is for servants. They don't even register as people to Daya.

"Master is upset with me," he warbles out. Probably for something stupid, like a crease in a napkin.

"I'm sorry, he's a dick that way." He smiles at my wording and then drops the petticoat entirely and moves closer to me. "I'm Keri, what's your name?"

"Kip," he answers shyly.

Isn't he adorable?

"Well, Kip, I've pissed off the 'master,' so I'm stuck in the room for the night. You're welcome to hang out with me. I doubt anyone will look for you here." Decidedly calmer, I hide the riding outfit under the bed and grab a nightgown out of the dresser. I'm washing his shit blood off me since with only two guards without necklaces I can't go anywhere yet. No matter how mad or scared, I am.

Taking a quick shower, I find Kip cleaning my room. I tuck the knife and square of bloody dress, in the pocket of the gown, and sit on the bed to watch him. I know from experience if I try to help, it'll offend him, and having an ally or even a friend in this place is something I can't afford to screw up.

He's fast like all Brownies are, and within minutes the room—including the closet—is neat as a pin. When he's finished, he stops at the end of the bed and looks up at me.

"Do you have a Brownie?" he asks shyly. His little cheeks as red as apples.

"I have a whole family of them, they have a house of their own too," I answer with a small smile, thinking of Gertie and her family.

"Whoooa, you gave them a house?"

"I did... Kip, where's your family?"

"Mum didn't make the master's tea right, she didn't come back," he answers sadly, plucking at his bottom lip with a finger. Kip is incredibly childlike, but I don't think he's a child anymore. "Can I go with you when you escape?" he asks excitedly.

"Yes, and even if I don't escape, you can go to my home." I rattle off the address and watch his face as he digests it. Brownies have this incredibly precise ability to get to any address given to them. "Gertie is my head honcho. She'll look after you."

"You'll give me a home?" I nod, and when the pounding comes on the door, I push him under the bed and flick the blanket hanging down to cover him. I didn't expect them to come, but I should've. The shower was a waste of my time.

The zombie guards come in and grab me off the bed and drag me from the room. At first, I fight them, but no matter how hard I hit or bite or kick, they continue dragging me unerringly towards the door. I go limp in their grip as I'm hauled down the stairs and then down another. This is a place I haven't been before, and that doesn't soothe the anxiety clawing at me.

I'm in trouble, so much trouble.

Daya is waiting on us and turns to me with that same sadistically calm smile, except this time there's also a look of disappointment on his face as he says, "It seems that you're not very thankful for the luxuries and opportunities I'm providing for you. Once you have an attitude adjustment, I think that you'll see things more clearly." My heart rate increases, and I start to fight again against the guards who hold me in a punishing grip.

Beyond Daya is a marble table, and on the four corners of it are cuffs. It's a bloodletting table, and Faerie knows what else he does with it. I claw, bite and punch and the guards, in a state of near panic. The temptation to call their fate is strong—they're the same two guards I stole the necklaces off —but common sense rears its head, and I decide against it. It's my ace in the hole, and Daya will stop me before I can get out the door.

That doesn't mean I'm going to that table willingly. Dropping my weight altogether, I land in a crouch and sweep the legs of the guard on the right out from under him. His grip loosens enough for me to shake him off and turn to the other one. A quick punch to the throat relaxes his grip as he grabs his throat. So they *can* feel pain. I turn to run, free of their grasps, and magic seizes me in its unbreakable hold. Death magic.

"No!" I refuse to beg, but I can deny it all day long. I fight against the magic and push myself to the point I see black spots in my vision. Still, inch by inch, I'm pushed towards the table. When the cold stone touches my back, I look at Daya.

"One day... soon, I will kill you *father*, but first, I'll take everything you hold dear," I threaten through my clenched teeth. "All your power, your fine clothes, and fancy houses. And you'll be the one crawling and begging when I call the fate you've earned by all the suffering you've caused!"

He comes close to me and leans down to look in my face. "You share those detestable bloodthirsty traits of your mother. As *my* child, you should know your proper place and act with decorum and elegance. I will beat them into you if I have to." He flattens his palm against my chest, pushing me down with hardly any effort. I have no defenses against death magic, and he wields it like the weapon it is.

The invisible hands of magic move the cuffs around my ankles and wrists. Bound, frustrated, and a little terrified, I scream out my frustration.

"I don't want to do this, but your behavior leaves me no choice, daughter," Daya explains patiently, that discomforting ever-present smile on his face. "You will do as I wish and fulfill the reason for your creation, one way or another."

When the pain starts, I close my eyes and picture the faces of the people I love. As the pain ratchets up and screams leave my throat, their faces swim before me, and I let the scalding heat of tears leak down the side of my face as I pray to Faerie to protect them.

I WAKE UP NAKED AND STUCK TO THE SHEET OF MY BED. Peeling myself carefully off it, I shuffle into the bathroom and take a hot shower. Even as it burns the wounds all over my body, I grit my teeth and take it. Grabbing the washcloth, I scrub away the sick feeling of his touch on my body, and I refuse to leave any traces of it. They weren't even sexual touches—I hope—just punishing ones. A slice of a knife in a sensitive place, the burn of a hot iron in the bend of my knees. A cut inflicted by magic across my chest. He paid particular attention to the brands on my body too.

I hate the man more than I hated my mother, and I didn't think that was possible.

When the water runs clear, I step out of the shower and wrap a towel around myself. Kip is standing at the end of the bed with a shirt and a pair of shorts in his hands. Where he found them, I don't know, but I take them gratefully and let him help me put them on. Moving is painful, and my body is starting to stiffen from the trauma inflicted upon it.

My hands clench into fists at my sides. I haven't felt this type of emotion since my mom was alive, and the reminder doesn't make me feel anything but more hatred. Seething, stomach churning hatred. It's the first time in my life I've felt this way about someone else so intensely, and I'm not sure how that will change me. Hopefully, not in a way that I resemble either one of them.

Limping, I cross to the window. A caravan of cars is trailing down the winding driveway to the imposing stone gate standing guard at the entrance. Daya's bright red car is among them. It's a blatant display of wealth and power, possessing cars. They're a real rarity in our world. Daya might talk of decorum and other bullshit, but he's also a total snob who likes to toss around his importance.

A tug of energy starts at my toes and works its way up my body until I'm pacing, and then I stop and stare at Kip. He's my ace in the hole. "Kip, do you want to leave here?" He nods enthusiastically. "Okay, I need you to take the necklaces off the guards so I can use my magic, and we can leave this place." He stares at me, mute for several minutes.

"And I can still stay with you?" A homeless Brownie is prey to most Fae, so I completely understand his need for reassurance. One I have no problem giving.

"Yes, you can stay with me." He smiles again and teleports out. When he returns about ten minutes later, he has a handful of necklaces gripped in his little fist. "Okay now to my house at the address I gave you and wait for me. Tell Gertie that I sent you, and she'll get you settled." With a nod, he disappears.

Right, time to start the party.

When I open the door, the two guards stationed outside turn in unison to look at me, and without pause I whistle. This time the magic tears from me, a purple, fast moving fog that's visible to the naked eye. The purple tendrils weave around the men in choking vine-like tentacles and this time I don't watch what will happen. I simply will it to pass and start walking. With my goal clear in my mind, I ignore the burning of the brands appearing all over my body, some hurting more viscously than others.

This is the cost of my freedom, and I accept it gladly.

The whistling turns into singing, and as I make my way towards the front door, guard after guard comes for me. They never make it to me; instead, I continue to walk unhindered, leaving a trail of disaster behind me.

There's the smell and heat of a fire. The growls and roars of animals. Crashes and screams of pain. Frankly, I don't care what I'm calling forth. Focused on my goal, my magic lashes out from me, and the door splits down the middle and splinters outwards, aging as it crumbles to the ground in pieces. I pick my way through the doorway and keep walking forward. People rush at me from outside, and my song increases as they fall before me like dominoes, and I still don't care.

When I get to the ward, I push my hands against it and yell out the words of its destruction. Pushing my magic against it as hard as I can. It shivers and fights me, but I channel all of my anger, my hurt, through my hands. With a final shudder, it drops with a clang of bells. The alarm of its demise.

Daya will know his wards are down, but by the time he gets back, I'll be gone.

Running now, I speed through the woods, pushing my body past the point of exhaustion. I'll pay for this later, potentially with my life, but I can't stop until I'm away from this place and the man who sits on its macabre throne. I'd rather die from exhaustion then stay another day in that place, living at the whim of someone who doesn't understand what love is and only twists and morphs it into something vile.

When the jarring abrasiveness of concrete beneath my feet registers, it brings me out of the panicked haze that's kept me going for miles. Stopping, I'm breathing heavily as I stagger towards the first house I see. When I pound on the door, a green-haired Fairy woman answers. I send a silent thank you to Faerie for this miracle. Her bright amber eyes search my face, and then when she sees the marks, she pulls me inside and shuts the door.

"What has happened to you?" she asks, steering me towards a chair at her small table.

I open my mouth to tell her to call Ciar and collapse.

## CHAPTER 5
## A FAIRY TO THE RESCUE

The murmur of voices pulls me to painful consciousness. Laying there with my eyes closed, I listen to the hum of conversation around me. Fairy or not, I can't be too careful, but the fact that I'm still at her house instead of back at Daya's is a good sign.

"She has two marks which automatically tells me that our kind protects her, but she passed out before I could get any information from her. Fortunately, I recognized one of them as your mark and got word to you as soon as I could." There's a pause, and I feel more than one gaze on me. "She's in bad shape, Bis... really bad. Death magic made most of those wounds, and they're not healing, then you have to take into account the brands that are all over her," the Fairy woman whispers. But I'm already past that. Bis is here, and my life or death struggle doesn't matter. I'm only one step away from home.

Pushing myself up slowly to rest on my elbows, I look over at him. He's already looking at me and walking towards me.

"Ah, sweet Keri, what has happened to you?" he says, kneeling on the floor at my side.

"Home Bis... please, take me home," I plead.

I don't have the energy to explain it all right now. His face softens even more, and without another word, he lifts me into his arms. With a murmured thank you to the Fairy for helping me, he begins to walk rocking me gently in his grasp. Feeling safe for the first time in weeks, I close my eyes and lean my head against his chest. The buzz of his wings surprises me, and any other time I'd have been ecstatic about flying with a Fairy, but this time all I know is the relief that I'm going home.

I must've dozed because it feels like only a few minutes have passed when my body dips into the softness of a familiar bed. *My bed.* My eyes open as the door thumps against the wall. Hard, green eyes soften when I meet them. Ciar. Behind him is Trick, his cyan eyes bright with worry.

Ciar takes one long look at me and is on his knees beside me a second later. When he hesitates to touch me, I realize I must look rough for the Puca to not grab me up in a hug. Smiling, I grab him instead, and he gently cradles me in his arms, his lips a soothing balm on my own. Kissing him seals the final need for reassurance, confirming my safety.

Ciar's mouth reluctantly leaves mine, and he looks into my eyes.

*I love you, Monster Girl.*

"Ya had us worried, Keri," Trick says, sitting on the bed at my legs. His hand strokes my calf softly, and his magic tickles my skin as he fights against the death magics with its claws still in me. Trick proves his strength because miraculously, he wins the battle and the pain eases for the first time since I walked out of Daya's place.

"I decided to rescue myself," I tease them in a hoarse voice. "You'd have never gotten me out of there, that entire place is anti-Faerie." Yawning from exhaustion, I give him a sleepy smile. Ciar gives me a soft smile on return and lays me back on the bed. "Did Kip get settled in okay?"

"Yes, Gertie is mommying him as we speak." Comforted, I let another worry go.

I'm only half surprised when he nudges Trick out of the way and crawls onto the bed with me. He pulls me onto his chest and wraps me in his arms, almost painfully tight—but I don't care. He's tense, and I know that he worried a lot more than he's letting on. To think that the Puca has come so far. Smiling into his shirt, I sigh in contentment. Another warm presence fills the space behind me, and a hand rests lightly on my lower back. I go to sleep to the soft hum of Ciar's voice against my cheek and the comfort of their warmth.

### Trick

"KEEP THAT ASSHOLE OUT OF HERE," CIAR SAYS WITH A coldness that gives me chills. He doesn't move from the bed; he hasn't budged since Keri fell asleep, and I imagine he won't until she wakes up. Something I can completely understand, but one of us has to get up and deal with the white-haired man hovering outside of the door.

Our girl is in bad shape, even using the strongest of my nature magic to rid her of the death magic clinging like a disease, still hasn't healed her as well as we hoped. Her face is a mass of cuts and bruises, her eyes are black and blue, and one is damn near swollen shut. That's not to mention the dozens of other injuries all over her body. All over.

The sadistic fucker tortured her. I know knife-work when

I see it. Methodical at that. That's not even counting the multitude of new brands all over her body.

I watch Rime hovering at the threshold with an angry look on his face. While I watch him, watching her sleeping, a multitude of emotions flash through his eyes. When they settle and alight with something familiar—and worrisome—to me, I move to stand in between him and the bed.

I haven't seen it for a long time, but I'd recognize it anywhere. Mania.

Out of all of the emotions he went through, I can't fault that I saw love mixed in there too. If he loves her, then why the facade with the bond? None of his behavior is making sense to me. I had planned on letting Keri deal with him, but sudden anger drives me toward the snowman. Rime's eyes widen as he backpedals into the hallway. I shut the door quietly behind me and stalk towards him. Ciar isn't the only one who has a bit of animal in him. I have them *all* in me.

"Tell me the damn truth now you git, or I'll kick your ass to tomorrow and deal with the consequences later," I threaten, poking a finger into his chest. His magic rises to meet mine, but the smell of forests weave around me and renders his useless. Ciar has my back it seems, not that I needed it.

"That's the real her?" he asks stupidly.

I've never cared for the man, not since the first time I met him, he acts like a man-child with an incredibly fragile ego—but I was willing to overlook my dislike for Keri's sake. That's not the case any longer.

How dare he look at her with anger after what she's gone through!

"Yes, and until you get your shit together, you'll stay well away from her."

"Trick." The anger flows out of me as quickly as it built.

Her speaking my name can turn me into a calm mute. It's a disconcerting feeling but not an unwelcome one. I've waited a long time to meet her, to love her, and I'm not about to let something as stupid as my pride get in the way of being with her.

A shiver runs through me as she lightly runs her fingers down my spine. Without another word, I step back and allow her to walk—limp—around me to confront Rime. This is not what I expected from her, especially considering the shape she's in. Then again, she likes to surprise me.

That doesn't stop me from trying to read her thoughts, and I could before this all happened. My cursory feelers are met by a stonewall of silence. I stop while I'm ahead. She might not be thrilled I'm trying to intrude. I can always ask her later.

The emotions chase themselves across Rime's face, once again, like a bunny running from a predator. He cares about her, truly, but there's more on his face than that. Guilt, fear, and in the end, that eerie light of mania returns to his eyes.

"Rime, what's going on?" Her voice is soft, but there's a steel thread underlying it that makes it a demand that won't be denied.

He opens his mouth several times and closes it, until finally he sighs in annoyance and says, "In one of my first incarnations, I made a mistake with a woman—she was beautiful, and I thought myself in love... but I wasn't. Unfortunately, she was a powerful Fairy and cursed me. Every time I fall in love, I lose my sanity. Every life without fail, I go crazy and die prematurely."

"How did you bond with me, Rime?" she asks calmly, not giving away how distraught she is. At least to someone not looking for it.

"He promised me an end to the curse. All I had to do was

to meet you, charm you, and use the magical push he gave me to bond with you."

"The pregnant woman?" Her voice is barely above a whisper, but we both hear her clearly.

"A part of the plan—I needed a way to appeal to your soft side. Daya mapped out everything, including the woman, and he was right with most of it." I can't see Keri's face, but as Rime speaks, her body tenses up tighter than a Leprechaun's purse strings.

"Why is the curse affecting you, Rime?"

"Why do you think, Keri? Because I was stupid enough to fall in love with you. As the days pass, it'll get worse and worse, and the only way to delay it is to *stop* loving you." He grimaces and runs a hand through his already messy hair. "When I fucked a woman in town last night... I tried everything to stop thinking about you. Nothing worked; every time I looked at her, I saw your face. I've even tried hating you, but the only thing I can use is the anger of this entire mess." He gives her a twisted smile and continues, "I don't regret agreeing to help him, because he can do something about this curse that's plagued me for so long. I do regret that you'll get hurt in the process." Every word out of his mouth makes her physically flinch.

He's not doing anything but blaming her for not letting him use her to get his reward. What a cunt.

My fingertips rest on her lower back, and when she leans back against them, I see how much this is hurting her but also sense that stepping in is the wrong thing to do. She wouldn't be working so hard to keep her composure if she wanted us to say anything to Rime.

Rime continues in a suddenly snide voice, "He said all I had to do was bond with you and bring you to him when he requested, and he'd fix everything. I want a normal life Keri, more than I even want you. I didn't expect the complications of being with you, caring about you. When he made the offer, I figured it was a job and nothing else. Now it has the potential to drive me to my death once again before I've even gotten to live."

My poor Keri girl, if he keeps running his mouth, I'm going to risk her wrath and rip the lips off his face. "Please understand, Keri. This curse makes me go mad and die within a few months of the onset. I've dealt with it for hundreds of years, and I can't take it anymore. This was my guaranteed chance of someone removing it and giving me freedom." His face becomes more earnest as he asks for her forgiveness and maybe even to hand herself back over to Daya, but Keri's posture doesn't relax. If anything, the clenching of her fist at her side tells me she's angrier at him for pleading than for being a flat out twat in the beginning.

She's hurt, yes, I can feel it radiating off her, but the level of anger surprises me. She's always had a streak of extreme patience when it comes to Rime, giving him understanding and softness when sometimes he didn't deserve it. That's no longer the case.

What did that twisted fuck of a father do to her while she was gone?

"Keri?" Rime questions, stepping towards her.

In a movement too fast for me to catch, she punches him in the face, taking him down to his knees. He looks up at her, kneeling like a guilty knight before his liege, with blood streaming from his nose. Without a word, she rears her leg back and kicks him as hard as she can in the balls. He goes crashing back into the wall, taking it and the table next to it down.

Bits of drywall and plaster fall on his head as he slides over to his side, his eyes closed.

"If you had told me, I'd have helped you, Rime!" she yells and turns to go back into the room. The door slams with enough force to reverb through the hallway. It immediately opens again, and she grabs me by the shirt and forcefully pulls me in the room. Leaning around me, she says, "Rime, be gone in the next five minutes, or I'm sending Fluffy after you." Rime's laying on his side on the floor, gaping at her.

I swear to Faerie he has hope in his eyes that she'll help him, but whatever look is on her face when she meets his eyes is enough to kill that hope. He looks... defeated. She slams the door again and pushes me towards the bed.

Ciar has his head propped up on his arms and looks mighty annoyed.

"Are you sure about this, Keri? I know you love him," Ciar asks as she slides back into bed with him. His tone of voice is calmer than the anger in his eyes. Ciar is better at faking it than I am.

"The only thing I'm sure of now is the need to sleep more. I'll deal with reality when I wake up." She snuggles against him and shuts her eyes. In her opinion, the conversation is on hold, but not in mine.

When she begins to snore lightly, a sure sign of her exhaustion, Ciar speaks again, to me this time. "We need to rebond with her, all of us, except for Rime."

I sit on the end of the bed, close enough to touch her leg, noticing for the first time how dirty her feet are. "That includes Bael?" I consider getting a wet cloth and washing her feet, but it'd probably wake her up, and people only go to sleep that fast when they're past the point of exhaustion.

"Yes, we need her Triad solid, and I think with him, it will be more so than it has ever been. It explains why our power didn't 'level up,' so to speak," he explains. "She's been drawn to him from the beginning even as she was repelled; it's why I assured her that a Triad can be more than three bonds. It's rare, super rare, in fact, but it has happened. I didn't start growing concerned about ours until right before she was taken... I thought perhaps it was delayed because the two of you have only exchanged blood and not completely tied the bond, but I was wrong."

"She's a stubborn thing, all mouth and bluster, but this messed her up Ciar. And when you throw a broken heart in the mix, complications will arise that we're not equipped to deal with." I look down at her dirty feet again. "But, we'll definitely be completing the bonds."

"Keri is one of the strongest people I know. We'll help her through this, and she will come out stronger on the other side. It's how she's wired," Ciar explains, and I believe him. He's known her most of her life. I'm still learning all of the nooks and crannies of her personality.

"Have you told Zag or Fluffy yet?" Not that I know how to tell the giant worm anything. He doesn't exactly talk.

"They're both sleeping under the bed. Zag didn't want Fluffy to wake her," Ciar answers with a bit of amusement.

Chuckling, I shake my head; it figures.

"His fat ass would've tried to lay on her, under the bed was the most logical choice," Zag says, his voice muffled by the bed. "And I agree with the bonding, and I'm also considering that eating Rime might be a good solution... someone should. Whether he cares about her or not, he just hurt her more than her father ever could." There's a huff followed by silence.

This might be the only time that all of the men— excluding snowflake—are in agreement. Shame she isn't awake to witness it. I look around, wait—there is one missing.

"Where did Bael go?" I ask, in general.

"He followed Rime out. He was lurking in the hallway behind him the entire time."

"Fuck, he's as creepy as you are," I mutter. Ciar chuckles as I head downstairs, she'll be hungry when she gets up, and I have to spend the next hour talking Gertie into letting me cook for her.

# CHAPTER 6
## GOOD NEIGHBORS

When I finally drag myself from the nothingness that is thankfully my dreams, my growling stomach reminds me that it's been days since I've eaten anything. Rolling over onto the bed that's cooled despite the fact that I know Trick was behind Ciar and me virtually under me at some point, I enjoy the comforting knowledge of where I am.

I'm home.

As I stretch my muscles and various painful spots protest. I flinch as a scab pulls across my back. Slowly sitting up, the smell of unwashed body wafts towards my face, and I grimace. That smell is coming from me.

Hobbling into the bathroom, I take a warm, long shower, staying in it until the water runs cold and makes me shiver. When I get dressed and go downstairs, the smell of bacon draws me to the kitchen, but a knock at the door stops me halfway.

I know who's knocking, I can *feel* him there like little bees buzzing near my skin. Bael is standing on the other side as aware of me as I am of him. I open the door to find him leaning against the frame, looking as nonchalant and hot as ever. But it's his eyes that pull me in. They're intent on me and the arrogance I usually see in them, although present is tempered by a much softer light.

A strangely pleasant surprise.

"What are you doing here?" Although I already know—have known for a while now.

"You already know why." I want to hear him say it, so I wait. Sure, it's a silly game to play, but I think at this point, I'm entitled to act silly. "You need a solid Triad, and I want—no, need to be a part of it and your life." That was not what I was expecting to come out of his mouth. He's put a lot more thought into this than I ever expected him to. Color me impressed.

With a smirk like he knows what I'm thinking he continues, "Daya won't stop, we both know that and your Puca, no matter how powerful he is—can't fight him. With me part of your real Triad," Oh, he knows about that part, huh? "My contribution should be enough to protect you more thoroughly."

A million different thoughts churn in my mind, but my mouth has other ideas. "Fine, but don't expect to jump into bed with me yet."

Bael smiles wide, and as I frown, I ask him why. "Because you said *yet*." Oh, that.

Rolling my eyes I shut the door in his face and then realizing what I did, mostly out of habit, open it back up and say, "I realize you live next door, but you might want to move here, you can have—" My mouth dries, and I can't bring myself to say *his* name, swallowing I continue, "You can have the now empty bedroom." Then I shut the door again in his face.

"Keri, you need to choose a Patron, I can't stave off my father much longer—not even by being part of your Triad," he says through the door.

"I know, Bael. Go pack before I change my mind," I reply after several beats of silence. Knowing I need a full Triad and that one member—I rub my chest as an ache slices through it —is gone, doesn't make things easier. Heartbreak hurts, no matter how strong you are, but it also eases as time passes too. And one day, another might fill the void left behind.

I don't have to be in a hurry to make that happen and won't either.

But emotions won't cloud the need or the presence of the person who will fill that empty spot. I refuse to allow Daya to retake me, and Bael's addition to our group will hopefully prevent that or at least make it much more difficult.

I've seen my meshed fate with Bael, I know one day it will happen—fate's a bitch that way, but the rest of it doesn't have to be tomorrow. The bond will be enough for now.

"You're thinking hard about something, eh?" Trick asks, startling me.

Heart still racing, I attempt to smile at him, but it falls flat. I don't feel like smiling right now.

"I told Bael to move in."

"Ah, bet that was a fun conversation," he muses, looking over me carefully. He's such a softie. I didn't know that until this moment. He and Ciar don't deserve to deal with the emotional backlash that snowflake has caused. They deserve the love and commitment they've earned.

The smile returns to my face, real this time, and I loop my arm through his and pull him towards the kitchen. Food is calling, and I'm not about to pass up on bacon.

CIAR HASN'T RETURNED FROM HIS HUNT—I'M ASSUMING it's a hunt—so breakfast was only Trick and myself. He kept heaping food on my plate until I eventually had to have

Gertie take the remaining food away or pop. Now he's sitting there with his elbows on the table watching me like I'm going to fall apart.

"I'm fine, Trick," I say, breaking our comfortable silence.

"I'm allowed to worry," he says, eliciting a bit of moosh from me. I think in all the mess with bonding with Rime—a mistake it seems—and everything else I didn't take the time to get to know the enigmatic man in front of me. Perhaps it's time to rectify that.

"What did you gentlemen get up to while I was... indisposed?" I ask, sitting back in the chair to give my overfull stomach more room to breathe.

"Oh, a bit of this and that. Mostly mild panic. Your plan worked out much better than ours. We were going to hold their toilet paper and other essentials hostage. Figured with as snooty as Daya and his gang are they'd give in rather quickly."

A soft laugh escaping surprises me. "I'm sure they would've caved in to your demands. Who can live without toilet paper in such a posh palace?" Thoughts of my recent stay at Daya's house makes me shiver. I refuse to let it knock me down completely, but I can't stop it from giving me a jolt of apprehension.

Ciar's presence washes over me like a warm bath. When he slides into the chair beside me, I look at him but otherwise don't react. He leans one arm on the table and gives me an impish smile as he slides my bracelet across the table to me. The handsome devil that he is knows how to distract me from the path my thoughts were trying to take.

"Has the worm accosted you yet?" When I shake my head, he continues, "I'm surprised he's not wrapped around you like a leech, poor thing missed you. What about your Dragon kitty?"

"I'll have you know, Puca, I'm more than capable of

making a snack out of you," Zag announces as he lands a few inches from me on the table. Leveling his head with my face, his tongue flicks out and tickles my cheek. Those swirling dark eyes hold mine as he sends me love and affection, curling back a lip he darts his head forward and nips at my chin.

The sting is nothing compared to what I've more recently experienced, so I don't even flinch. The bond reforming is like a steel beam of love that latches onto my soul and heart and gives me room to breathe for the first time in weeks.

Grabbing him, I pull him to me and hug him like a teddy bear. He protests, mildly and without heat, and snakes his head into my hair where he sighs in contentment. My dragon missed me as much as I missed him.

"I will not let anyone take you again from me, ever," he whispers into my hair. His words make me hug him tighter until he squeaks in complaint, and I release him. He sits back on his haunches and turns his head to look at Ciar and then Trick. "Well, get on with it. She needs your strength."

He's talking about our bonds. Sitting up, I frown and say, "Zag... both of them at once?"

"As if that'll be an issue," he mutters, turning my concern into a different type of meaning. Throwing my head back, I laugh. It's unexpected and wonderful.

Zag huffs and says, "One at a time, and don't forget that other Fae." He turns to look me in the eyes. "I know this will be hard on you, but it's the best protection."

"It's okay Zag, I'll be fine, but I don't think all three—" Something large bumps my leg and then the weight settles on my lap, I look down at Fluffy's many eyes and catch myself laughing again. "Make that four. Fluffy, go first." I hold my hand near one of his mouths, and he gently nicks me with one pincer like tooth. I hug his head to me too.

Two things are right in the world again. I look at Ciar

expectantly then realize what it could mean picking him first, so I turn to Trick to explain.

"Trick—" I start to say.

He cuts me off. "Keri, you never have to justify anything like that to me. Bond with twinkletits there, and then we'll renew ours when you're ready," Trick says, hooking a thumb at Ciar.

"And Bael?" Just saying his name makes my heart rate pick up, and although it annoys me, I can't deny that bonding with Bael feels like the right thing to do even if I was tricked once before.

Then again... I don't seem to have the same reluctance that I did with Rime. It's for a different reason entirely. Even though Ciar is as powerful, probably more so than Bael, I've known Ciar most of my life. Bael, I've known for months, and we have yet to sit down and have a normal conversation. I know next to nothing about him other than he's the King's son and has developed an interest in me.

At least now, I know why. He felt the pull before I realized what it was before I knew that Rime was never supposed to be part of my life.

"Keri," Ciar says to get my attention. I look up at him questioningly. He pounces and swoops me up in his arms; naturally, I wrap my arms around his neck and my legs around his waist. My Puca has been as patient as he's capable of being, and with him, I can let go.

"Time to show you that you're mine, Monster Girl," he says against my cheek before his lips touch mine, and I'm lost. The gentle rocking makes it obvious we're moving despite the fact he has yet to stop kissing me, but I'm not worried about falling. He won't let me.

The low growls in his throat make the hair on the back of my neck stand, and I kiss him harder. Ciar will never, ever hurt me, but he's more monster than man, and I know that he needs to reforge the bond and maybe make both of us forget what happened. I'm okay with it.

The bed cradles my back, and with his lips still on mine, my clothes start to disappear. Carefully he removes them, achingly slow, his eyes open and holding mine. They're slightly squinted in concentration as he continues to devour my mouth and baby my injured body.

I'm not as considerate of myself.

Fighting his hold, I pull away from him and grab the collar of his t-shirt, meeting his eyes I pull it until the soft material gives way in my hands. His green eyes light up, and a smile lifts the corner of his mouth, conveying his permission to continue. He's propped on his knees with his arms supporting his weight. His hands grip the sheet on either side of me, and I know that what I'm doing is affecting him as much as it is me. I'm nearly panting with desire for him.

Almost in a frenzy, I destroy the rest of his clothing as I remove it—rip it really—from his body and behold the glory of the man who somehow fell in love with me. A fact I know to be true; I can see it shining brightly in his eyes as he watches my face for even the minutest change in expression. They flick from side to side, resting briefly on my mouth before he does the sexiest thing ever, he licks his bottom lip.

Just the tip of his tongue sliding over it has the ability to make me wet enough to be slightly embarrassed. But my Puca won't let me stay that way. With a growl, he divests me of any sense of time or place as he kisses my neck, each mark on my chest, and then finally takes one of my aching nipples in his mouth.

Moaning, I bury my hands in his hair, tight enough to probably hurt him, but when his teeth lightly nip at me I know he likes it.

"Bond... Ciar, before my vagina takes over my brain," I breathe out.

With a chuckle, he moves his mouth to the top of my breast, hovering over a cut that Daya inflicted. Eyeing me with possession in his gaze, his teeth elongate and sink into my skin. Instead of pain, pure pleasure shoots through me, and some of the trauma that came with my wounds eases. Raising his head he runs his tongue over a sharp tooth, piercing it and pooling blood in the dip of his tongue as he leans down and lathes my lips and tongue with it.

The bond awakens with an explosion of the senses as euphoria stretches and overtakes every cell of my body. I cry out his name, and the last words I remember uttering are... I love you.

# CHAPTER 7
## THE SWEATY MAMBO

Sweaty and completely sated, I roll over onto Ciar's hot, equally sweaty body. He's on his back with his eyes closed, a full-blown smile on his face. Staring at him, I run my finger over his small nipple, and he chuckles when I repeat it to get a reaction.

"Do you want more, Monster girl?" he teases, knowing full well that after *three times,* I'm done for a while. Parts of my body are sore from his touch and teeth but in a good way. The overwhelming haze of the bond has finally dimmed, and my body is letting me know in no uncertain terms that no matter what I'm thinking in my head about how beautiful he looks laid out like a feast for the senses, I'm not ready quite yet.

"I missed you—every single minute. There were times that I felt like a failure as your mate because I couldn't force my way in there and save you. I plotted, I threatened, I killed trying to discover any way I could to get you out. But you were," his eyes open and meet mine, "so far away from me, and if something had happened to you..." His words trail off, but I know what he's saying without saying it.

Ciar is a proud man but not so prideful that he can't

admit that without me, he'd not want to go on. There's a sense of a second heartbeat inside of me. My Puca is back where he belongs, tied to my soul and I'll fight to the death to keep it that way.

"I love you, Keri. More than anything, anywhere... ever. With a bond, without one, I will continue to love you. I fell in love with who you are, the way you laugh. The determination you have to overcome everything and still retain that sweet, lovely humor of yours has always been an admirable quality about you. Don't let that bastard take that light in your soul away."

My eyes burn, and tears leak out to drip onto his chest. With a soft smile he wipes them away and pulls me to him.

"I thought it was because you liked my ass," I tease, feeling that spark of humor flair to life.

"Oh, I love that too." Which he demonstrates by cupping it with one of his big hands. He kneads it and pulls me against his arousal. Randy bastard is ready to go again. Laughing, I kiss him and slide my hand down his stomach to wrap my hand around it. Stroking it, I watch his face and smile again when his breath hisses out, and his eyes widen with pleasure.

Being able to affect a man such as he so drastically will forever please me. He bites his bottom lip and my skin tingles.

"Oh, fuck it," I mumble, climbing on top of him.

His laugh is cut off as he slides inside of me. *Take that, Ciar.*

Ciar

SHE'S ALWAYS SLEPT LIKE A CHILD, ARMS THROWN OUT, mouth hanging open as her feet and hands twitch along with whatever dream her devious mind cooks up. Tonight she lays curled up at my side. Her knees tucked tight against my hip, her head burrowed into my shoulder. One hand is fisted in the sheet over my stomach, and the other one is locked around my arm, anchoring me in place. There's a frown on her beautiful face as well.

Daya wounded her in more ways than one. It makes me want to kill him more, something I didn't even know was possible. Knowing she was in his grasp and I could do nothing to save her unmanned me in a way that I'm still reeling from. I *failed* her. I failed the love of my life when she needed me the most.

It wasn't just Daya. Rime's betrayal took a lot out of her. She was slow to come around, but she came to love him despite the weakness of the bond. A pure kind of love that the fool should feel privileged to have directed at him. Instead, he's so wrapped up in ending his curse. He doesn't see the extraordinary thing that comes along once in a lifetime.

He didn't give her a chance to help him. Not that he belonged in the bond to begin with. Daya tainted it all with his meddling, poisoning something that could've been real despite the false beginning. She would have remained bonded to him and welcomed Bael in as well. She was holding Rime close to her because her love was real.

Love that is twisting and turning inside of her and slowly but surely severing itself in her heart. But at what cost to Keri?

With a light touch, I tuck a piece of hair behind her ear and run my finger down her cheek. Being bonded with me again has sped up her healing, and the wounds that were so grievous hours ago are now starting to heal. The large bruises that marred an entire half of her face have faded to a mottled yellow color and will be completely gone in the morning.

So the physical injuries will soon be gone, leaving the emotional ones behind.

We lay and talked for hours until her yawns became so frequent that she passed out in this position. A defensive one. She steadily avoided talking about Rime, no matter how I tried to broach the subject. I can't heal her broken heart, only she and time can, but I can make it easier for her. Trick will play his part as well. And I can't forget the familiars that snuck into the room the minute she passed out. Zag is curled up near her head, and Fluffy is weighing the bed down on the far side, a multitude of his legs touching her for reassurance.

I'm not the only one to suffer from her absence, and no matter how selfish I want to be with her, that's not the life we live.

Gertie and her family have popped in to check on her several times but are waiting for Keri to come to them. They don't want to intrude on our rejoining. The Fairies are hovering as well, and I can't fault them for it. If not for the marks and Bis... she'd not be here.

Rime needs to be dealt with, Bael followed him and shared that Rime went to stay at a priest enclave. Donn's priests. Rime is a conundrum; I saw the love he has for her, and it couldn't have all been from the bond. Rime isn't that good of an actor, and I know some of what he felt for her was real... just not enough. He weakened our Triad, although now that Bael is here, we'll be stronger than ever. I wish it wasn't at Keri's expense.

She knows she needs to bond with Bael and is surprisingly not dragging her feet with it. Keri does have practicality when the situation calls for it. And despite my dislike of anything to do with the Fae kingdom, Bael is an excellent choice. He's already half in love with her, and given the quiet way he watches her, I feel that he has accepted his place in her life and has the patience to wait for her to welcome him into it.

Moving him into the house is a start—that I wasn't expecting. But I did share the vision she saw of them together. I even taunted him with it. Wrong of me sure, but he needs to understand, I'll share her, but I was first.

Keri makes a noise in her sleep, and I angle my body more towards her, pulling her closer with the arm I tuck around her, shielding her as best as I can from the dreams that plague her mind and heart.

The pull of the hunt becomes painful, but I ignore it. I won't leave her; justice can be had without me. The Sluagh do their jobs well. Tonight I'm holding her with no interruptions. Faerie will either punish me or forgive me for it, but I'm uncaring which one she chooses.

Tomorrow we'll talk about the Dark Forgetful Forest. Faerie wants me to claim the crown, the cost of the boon she gave me, and I need to find a way to protect Keri when I'm so damn helpless against Daya.

Suddenly I smile, my teeth so sharp they tear into my lips.

Only Daya is protected from me. Donn's influence goes no further. Tomorrow I'll do more than Faerie's hunt.

## CHAPTER 8
## DADDY'S GIRL

When Ciar told me we're making a trip to the Dark Forgetful Forest, I got so excited I cried. Maybe some of it is because I get to see Nagan. He's my father in every sense of the word, and I think I need to overwrite the messed up 'love' from Daya.

I need my daddy.

Packing is quick, and I stop long enough to hug Gertie, who's holding herself away from the group, wringing her hands in worry. She cries a moment into my shoulder and says, "Go on with you now. I'll have a lovely dinner ready when you get home in a few days." I kiss her cheek and practically skip out to the wagon. Fluffy, who finally got to wrap himself around me like an overly long scarf, snorts happily as he crawls up the wagon and stretches out in the back. Zag huffs and plants himself on my lap.

He's been sticking close to me even though he's said nothing. The looks he gives me is enough, and like the other men in my life, he feels like he failed. They think I'm not sharp enough to figure that out. It's in their eyes every time they look at me. A sense of shame hangs gloomily around them, and I'm determined to fix it during this small spot of what I'm deeming a vacation.

I even invited Bael.

I chew on my lip. Is it wrong of me to let him into my heart when Rime has stabbed it so hard? I'm pulled towards him in a way that gives me no room to back off, and trying to keep him at arm's length seems stupid. Bael is genuinely supposed to be part of our family and in some ways has been cheated from experiencing that because of someone else... he deserves to be here, and I deserve to have someone who genuinely wants to be.

But damn does it still hurt. The only saving grace in all of it is our love was new; it hadn't sunk its roots deep into my soul like Ciar's has. I can live without Rime. I can move on without him too. Still hurts.

So Bael and Trick will have to wait a little longer for my heart. I can't love anyone else yet, not deeply. I just can't. Not until I get through it myself. That doesn't stop me from wanting to make them a more intimate part of my life. It needs to be done. We need our Triad strong. More importantly, I want to do it because they're two of three gorgeous men who will be spending the rest of their lives entangled with me.

And no one is going to break the damn bond again. No way. I might not have been keen on the bond in the beginning, but after sharing it with someone and then having it ripped away like that... *no one* will take it from me again. I don't care who it is. I'll stab them with rusty spoons. I'll pull their spleen out through their noses. Anyone who dares will suffer the wrath of—

"Why do I get the feeling you're thinking about killing people?" Ciar asks, a teasing glint in his eyes.

I clear my throat and point at the horses. "Make them

move, please." Laughing, he gives a gentle slap of the reins, and off we go.

As the miles go by, my excitement builds. The forest was my home for years, and I miss it all the time, but as happy and excited as I am to see my family I realize something profound too. My family is in this wagon, even Bael. *These* are the people that I go to when I want to feel safe and loved. These are the ones who are there for me every day.

They are my home now.

Subtly I wipe at the tears forming in my eyes and keep staring forward even though I know that three sets of eyes are on me.

"What are you three staring at? Can't a woman weep in peace without people gawking at her?" Zag demands from my lap. I'm torn between hugging him and flicking the top of his head.

"Way to call me out, Zag," I whisper. He turns his head and looks at me in surprise.

"Oh, well still, they stare at you like a bunch of slavering dogs," he whispers loudly back. When Trick chuckles behind me, I drop my chin to my chest with my hand over my face. Zag and I need to talk about personal boundaries. Regardless, I laugh, and it's one of those that starts at your toes and works its way out. And with it some of the horror left from Daya is let go.

Not all of it, but it's a good start.

"She is a tasty tidbit, Zag. I want to eat her up," Trick teases from behind me. I look over my shoulder at him with a smile on my face and wink. His eyes widen in surprise, but he recovers quickly and winks back. Out of the corner of my eye I see Bael's face too; there's a smile hovering on his mouth. Mister Fancy-Pants Duke has a sense of humor after all.

That's a relief.

"Oh, for Faerie's sake, you're all a bunch of heathens," Zag grumbles, but I know the Dragon well, and he did it all on purpose. I scratch under his chin, and he gives me a look. When he winks, I laugh again. Sneaky lizard.

Cuddling him a little, despite his half-hearted protests, I look in wonder at the scenery as we pass. There are large, rolling fields of crops lining the road we're traveling on. Tall rows of corn stretch for miles while on the other side, there are some green things I don't know the name of. The breeze is light and the day cool enough to require long sleeves, but the sun is bright and the sky a vivid blue with the silhouette of the moons always present, even during the day. There's not a cloud to be seen, and gazing at something so beautiful lifts my spirits even more.

Freedom feels good.

The air around us changes, and the smell of my childhood home entices yet another smile out of me. Trees, large and looming seem to spring from the ground as the road narrows, and the sounds of unknown creatures scuttling in the brush around us fill the air.

Sluagh appears out of the shadows and bushes to run along beside us, growling and roaring in greeting. Familiar faces make me call out in greeting, and I'm answered with one of them excitedly jumping over the horses. When one of the horses kicks out he makes a face and then smiles goofily as he runs ahead of us.

In the heart of the forest, fires of welcome greet us. At the side of the fire, facing us stands the tall, wonderfully familiar form of Nagan. Standing, I jump off the wagon while it's still moving, rolling stiffly to my feet but still getting them under me. Laughing I run towards the man who raised men and leap into his waiting arms.

The sob catches me off guard, but Nagan merely wraps his arms tighter around me and nickers soothingly in my ear. While I cry my heart out, my real father pats my back and smooths my hair, holding me like I'm a small child once again.

I needed this.

When I've cried myself out and become aware of just how quiet it is, I self-consciously pull away, and Nagan sets me on my feet. Cupping my face he wipes my tears away and smiles kindly.

"Hello, my girl," he greets. I cover his hands with my own.

"Hey, dad." His eyes widen in surprise for a split second, and then he puffs up with pride, clearing his throat to hide how pleased he is that I used the term. I pretend like I don't know what he's about.

Patting my head, he turns to wave me towards Mada's tree, standing tall and wide in the center of the village. She's resting against a root, watching me patiently with a smile of greeting on her face.

"Daughter of the forest, welcome home," she says, holding out her hand for me. I go to her willingly and let her embrace me as well, avoiding the crying this time, but it's a hard thing. The roughness of the bark of her skin presses against my back, and I welcome it. Mada is essentially the Dark Forgetful Forest.

"The forest welcomes you with open arms. It has missed you, Keri," she greets, smiling again. My answering smile is enough for her to raise her voice and announce the commencement of our celebratory dinner. When she claps her hands, clumps of dust fall from her arms, and I look away to hide my smile. She's incredibly self-conscious about her dusting.

Ciar's eyes catch mine, and the sheen of them in the light reminds me of many nights spent running from the big mutt in the forest. Training he said, I think he was having fun with it in hindsight. My eyes narrow when he smiles.

*Oh, the games we played, Monster Girl. You liked to tease me with dog jokes and offer me treats, chasing you was only fair.*

*What about when I was an adult?*

*I liked watching your ass.*

When I laugh out loud, Mada looks at me with an eyebrow raised. My lips purse and I debate telling her about our conversation then I remember that although kind to me, Mada has no sense of humor. At least not one like ours, hers tends to be rather dry and above my head most of the time.

As if she's reading my thoughts, she pats the root beside her, and of course, I sit. It's Mada after all.

"It is good tidings to see you well," she begins, observing my face. Her brown eyes are narrowed and go white while she's watching me. Mada sees something. "Ciar needs to capture his crown, and then he will no longer be a scion of Faerie; he will be part of her." The words are spoken in a monotone, with that faraway echoing voice her prophecies always carry.

I won't say it, but we already knew he needed to get his crown. That's an excellent way to piss her off, and I've experienced her temper enough in my life to want to avoid it. It's not that she's cruel, she's just creative. I had to pick up every red-stained leaf in the forest one summer as punishment. It took me the entire damn summer because they were all red.

"What do we do until then, Mada?"

She reaches behind her and picks off two pieces of bark. "Place these in places you are the most vulnerable, and Daya will not be able to get near you. No one will that you do not wish."

Mada never gives pieces of her tree to anyone, never in my life have I witnessed it. The fact that she gave it to me almost makes me cry all over again. She touches my cheek and smiles.

"You are the daughter of my heart, did you think I would

not want you safe?" Smiling sheepishly, I tuck the pieces of bark in my pockets and hug her again. "I tried to pierce his wards, but my magic was repelled. All I could do was wait for you to get into the forest and guide you to a kind soul." In shock, I turn to her. Mada left the forest and helped my mad dash through the woods outside of his house?

Tears do fall this time, and I feel like a right watering pot. She wipes them away, leaving smudges of dust on my face. I don't care though. "I would do anything for you, Keri."

There have been moments in my life where I felt the keen absence of a mother, but at this moment, all of that leftover hurt, and feelings of abandonment dissipates. I had one all along.

"Thank you, Mada... for everything," I grasp her hand when I say it, hoping she feels the emotions coming from me that I don't have the proper words to express. She pats my hand and slightly inclines her head; yeah, she understands me.

"You have collected yourself an interesting Triad, Keri. A King of Faerie, a Trickster, born of magic and a powerful Prince. Yet, I see that one is missing, and you have not mentioned him." Mada probably already knows but wants to hear me say it. Maybe even wants to force me to talk about it. Isn't that something mothers do?

"He hijacked the bond, Mada. He has a curse that makes him go insane if he falls in love and Daya made a deal to remove it if he bonded with me, he even gave him a way to bond with me."

"Is he going insane?"

"Yes," I answer automatically, being hit by the truth of it. He actually feels something for me, not that it matters now. There's no way I'd ever accept him back into my life, not after he came into it with Daya's help.

I might have forgiven him if it were him on his own. Might. No guarantees.

"You have that, at least. Perhaps one day, he'll realize the wrong he has done in his selfishness," she says with white eyes again. That doesn't bode well for Rime, not if Mada sees something. My broken heart wants me to ask her, but my angry mind stops me.

His fate is no longer tied to mine. I have to let him go.

"There are times when the heart is fickle, and unfortunately, the one who does love always suffers. If you like I'll stomp him into the ground, Keri," Nagan comments coming up beside us. I smile, can't help it. He's in protective-daddy mode.

"Na, he doesn't even deserve that. I kind of get where he's coming from, but that won't help me forgive or forget what he did. I have to move on from it. The third real member of my Triad is leaning on that tree over there looking like the awkward kid at the party," I say, pointing at Bael.

His eyes raise to mine, and he surprises me by rolling his, smirking in the process.

Fairyfarts, he can't read minds too, can he? Two of them are more than enough as it is. Trick because he's my Anchor and Ciar because... well, because he's Ciar. It looks like a test is in order. Looking directly in Bael's eyes I picture the vision I had of him, of us—together. *Naked.*

The memory makes me feel hot and cold at the same time; self-conscious, I look away when Bael doesn't respond with anything more than a questioning look. When I look at Ciar, I see the smirk on his face that tells me he did see what's in my mind. There's a look of pure mischief on his face when he turns to Bael and asks, "Do you have a freckle next to your nipple?"

Bael straightens and looks at him with both of his eyebrows damn near his hairline.

"Why?" Bael demands.

"So you do? Keri was licking it in her imagination," Ciar

says, turning back to the fire with laughter in his eyes. He doesn't even look guilty for throwing me under the wagon like that.

"Bad dog," I whisper. When his head shoots back up, I know he heard me. This time I laugh, and it eases the small spat of embarrassment of Ciar calling me out that way. I understand why he did it. He wants me to be happy. He wants me to laugh. He succeeded too.

"Children," Nagan says under his breath. One of my favorite pastimes as a kid was making Nagan uncomfortable. That hasn't changed.

"Wasn't just his nipple, Ciar. Make sure you tell him the whole truth!" I yell across the clearing. Ciar throws his head back and laughs while Nagan shuffles his hooves. Trick is beside Ciar laughing, and even Bael has a smile on his face.

As I watch him, he looks around and takes a bracing breath before crossing to sit at the space on the other side of Trick. Right where he should be. My embarrassment was good for something.

"How about you play for us, Keri?" Nagan asks, doing his best not to give the guys death looks. He's rather prudish for a Centaur. I lean over and kiss his cheek and hop down to join the guys.

Music is a big part of any Fae's life, and my powers prove that too.

Holding out my arm, the violin appears in my hand, and the guys stand to join me. The bow appears in my other hand and I stroke it once against the strings, the sound is magic itself, and when I wink at Ciar he catches my plan in my mind. Usually, we'd play something folky, Nagan loves old songs, but I think it's time to bring him into modern times.

Instruments appear out of thin air as Trick—picking up on our game when I start playing the first few notes of a famous pop song—adds to the beat. The piano booms in the silence, and when the soft notes of a flute join the mix with Ciar's voice matching it, we start really jamming.

The Sluagh start to clap along with the music, adding to the beat, and I start bopping my head as the magic rises, taking everyone with it.

Ciar sings like a dream, and I lose myself in the moment.

Lose a little bit more pain in the process too.

## CHAPTER 9
## A DAD'S ADVICE

After everyone has started to settle down for the night, mostly because they're intoxicated, Nagan and I are sitting semi-alone watching the fire burn down. I caught him tapping his hoof to one of the more popular modern songs we played tonight and haven't let him live it down since.

My dear father has a soft spot for pop music.

"I was supposed to be in a Triad," he says randomly. I'm leaning against his warm, hairy side and can feel his tension. I keep my silence and wait for him to continue to speak, "The call pulled me, and I went, but by the time I got there she had picked another—a man she wanted for his position. My Center was a Fae and wanted nothing to do with an Unseelie like me. I have never felt the call again, and have accepted that it won't happen."

"Doesn't mean you have to be alone, Dad," I say softly. "And you never know what life will throw at you. I've seen weirder things happen."

"That foolish man had something special, once in a life-time and all he cares about is himself. As callous as this sounds, I think it's best he's out of your life."

I speak from my heart when I say, "Do you think I can help break his curse?"

Nagan snorts and says, "No, a curse like that is only breakable by true love Keri, and as much as I love you, you weren't that for him if he remains cursed." He pats my head and continues, "A person like him can't see past his desires, no matter what excuse he gives."

"Still, he doesn't deserve to be in pain."

"Neither do you." Touché. "How do you feel about the Fae?"

"He's stupid powerful, probably close to Ciar's level in some ways. He's also arrogant and used to getting what he wants. But there's something about him that I like... besides his six-pack," I say the last part under my breath.

"He looks at you like the other two. That was something the other was missing. Rime looked at you like he wanted you, but not like you were everything." That's rather profound and something I didn't notice because I was too busy looking at Rime like *he* was everything.

"It's a good time of year to go swimming, Mada has held summer for your visit," he says entirely off-topic. Patting his side, I climb to my feet, swimming does sound good, and it was one of my favorite things to do.

No harm in revisiting happy moments in childhood.

With a look to the preoccupied three men that are all sneaking glances at me, which is flattering, I can't deny it. I slip off into the shadows, confident in my safety. No one can come after me here, not even Daya and his minions. I don't have to spend my visit looking over my shoulder, and the smile I can't shake off my face shows it.

When I hear the bubbling gurgle of the small stream that feeds the swimming hole, I start to jog. The surreal feeling of time going backward makes me hastily strip my clothes the minute the pool is in sight. I run at it full throttle and leap the minute my toes touch the water.

The cold water makes me gasp but laugh as I sink into its dark depths. There are so many good memories layering this place; even Ciar played here—as much as a sarcastic Puca can play. Rising to the surface, I'm not completely surprised when I see a shape heading towards me through the underlit waters.

The sensation of *knowing* him is sharp and when Trick surfaces, as a merman, I laugh so loud it echoes. His skin is an aqua blue, and there are cute little gills lining his neck and scales shining on his forehead and cheeks. His hair is a vivid blue and is slicked back from the water. When he smiles at me I see sharp teeth and laugh again.

"I couldn't help but follow you," he admits. "There's not been much time alone for us since this all began, and I thought maybe... you wouldn't mind me joining you."

"Come here, Trick," I say, beckoning him with a finger. He doesn't hesitate one bit, he swims right for me with a smile on his face, and I grab a breath of air before we go under and down into the depths.

His lips meet mine, hot in the cold water, and at first I freeze, but when he starts to pull away I grab the back of his head and hold him in place. No, no I won't let Rime's actions punish Trick. He didn't do anything wrong and deserves more, especially from me. The kiss deepens as if he knows my thoughts.

Slowly we rise to the surface our lips seemingly fused in passion that has truly never been explored between the two of us. As the cooled air kisses my skin I pull a few inches away from him and smile.

The Merman shape has receded, and the real Trick is looking at me with eyes that have always had the ability to give me goosebumps. Smiling in return, his hands slide up to cup my face, and the colors of his eyes take over the pupil.

"You're the most beautiful thing I've seen, Keri. I love you more than anything and am thankful I'm part of your life," I open my mouth then close it.

I'm not ready to return that particular sentiment, but one day I will be. It's something I know without a doubt. And it doesn't mean that he and I have to be standoffish. I care about him a lot actually, I'm just not ready to say the big three words. When his face changes to a sweeter smile, one filled with understanding and patience I realize he's been poking around in my head.

"It's harder to block you out, isn't it?"

"Sometimes, but you're getting pretty good at it," he answers honestly. Since he came to stay with me, he's pretty open about things. And given the recent deception I've experienced from people close to me, it's refreshing.

Peeling away the shields I keep in my mind, and I allow him unfettered access to my thoughts. He frowns as the tickle of him in my mind almost makes me giggle. Ciar is like a breeze on a hot summer day, while Trick is like a light rain. They're so different and yet so similar that I can't help but smile about it.

Ciar is close to us, guarding us more than likely or watching—because he likes that too. The bond between him and me is a humming live wire of energy that I find comfort in possessing once again. His amusement makes my heart lighter. He's fully aware of what I'm up to, and now, looking at Trick's face, I can see that my shapeshifting mate does too.

"It's time to fix the bond, Trick. You ready?" I ask him, my voice sounding all breathy and low. Well, my intentions for tonight are now known.

Trick chuckles and lightly kisses me before gently, so damn gently, biting down on my lip. He didn't get more than a drop of blood, but it's enough to make his eyes glow. To stir the bond to life. I guess it's my turn.

I kiss his cheek and then his ear and further down his neck. I rest my mouth on the dip of his shoulder before biting down as easily as I can. He deserves the same gentleness he gave me. When the first drop of his blood hits my tongue, the world spins, and the haze of the bond instantly turns me on. Not that I wasn't already.

It's not as potent as the first time, our bodies and minds recognize each other now, but it still packs a punch.

With a small growl in his throat, his mouth captures mine while his hands touch me everywhere. I close my eyes and sink into the feeling of him and let the wave of lust that hits me like a wagon full of Fairy Cakes take me away.

Trick isn't as aggressive as Ciar, but he's a bit of an animal in his own way. His touch is firm but not painful as he grips me in his arms and carries me to shore. When my back hits the soft sand, he's on me once again, and I welcome him with open arms.

He lowers his head and kisses the first new brand, and feather light kisses follow suit on every other one on my stomach and chest. When his mouth touches my pussy, I'm lost.

Moaning, I grab his hair and let my inhibitions go.

Big, warm hands gentle massage my shoulders as Ciar makes himself known. Sluggishly I open my eyes and look up at his upside down face. Smiling, toothy, and sexy he leans down and slides his tongue between my lips.

Trick moves his tongue faster between my legs, and when the orgasm slams into me, I moan into Ciar's mouth. He holds still, savoring each sound, each gasp. When he pulls away I lift my head trying to chase after those wondrous lips, but he smiles and continues to stare into my eyes.

Gentle hands push my legs further apart, and Trick slides

into me like he's always supposed to have been there. Trick's and Ciar's heads are only inches apart, and both of them are entirely focused on me.

I can't say I don't love the feeling.

When Trick begins to move in slow long strokes that instinctually make me wrap my legs around his waist, I get the treat of him leaning down to suck my nipple into his mouth. Ciar watches Trick for a moment and then leans forward to take the other one.

The different sensations of each mouth are enough to drive me even closer to the edge. Trick grinds against me, pushing deep, and I use my legs to raise my hips to meet him. He removes his mouth with a wet pop sound from my breast and spurred on by my whispered demands; he moves faster. Shifting to his knees he lifts my ass to push deeper inside of me.

Each thrust elicits a moan until all I can do is mutter gibberish as I feverishly beg for more.

When my orgasm starts, I'm beyond thought, beyond anything but the two men touching me, loving me. It cascades over me with sharp bites of pleasure. I scream into the night, and the last coherent thought I have is...

I do love him too.

## CHAPTER 10
## FOURSOME ANYONE?

Dawn is barely touching the sky when we wander back into the small village of the Sluagh. Slowing my walk, I take a minute to bask in the almost magical stillness. Dew has settled on the trees and plants around us giving the burgeoning sunlight a shimmering welcome. This time of day is magical in the forest; there's a hush that blankets everything, even the birds are still sleeping. I used to sneak out and watch the sunrise, just to experience this moment.

When I look at the fire, a wistful smile still on my face, I see Bael sitting there, stirring it with a stick. He has one elbow propped on his knee and has his chin resting on the palm of his hand. There's a small frown on his face, and on instinct I cross to him and sit beside him.

"Hey," I greet, shoulder bumping him. If he's going to be part of my life, he needs to get used to my weirdness.

"Good morning," he greets me, tossing the stick into the fire. He turns to me, and I see the knowledge of what Trick, Ciar, and I was doing in his eyes. It's not jealousy. His emotions are completely transparent. It's envy. I can't help but be a little flattered.

I also don't miss Ciar and Trick creeping off, both wearing amused smiles on their faces. Way to abandon me, guys.

Looking back at Bael, who's looking at me like I'm the best thing he's seen today, guilt swirls in my stomach. I like him; there's no denying that. I'm attracted to him too, but I'm going to push the bond early because I need a full Triad for what's coming.

"It's okay, you know," he says with a smile that's full of arrogance. How he pulls that off this early I'll never know.

"What's okay?"

"That for the moment, you're closer to them. I know my time will come." He's not wrong, so I don't argue. "Don't feel like you're using me either," he says, hovering his hand over mine somewhat awkwardly before finally grasping it and curling his fingers around it. "Until I saw you, I'd have never considered I would have a Triad, let alone be so fascinated with another person."

I'm flattered once again, and if that's his intent he's succeeding beautifully. That thought makes me smile, and he smiles in return.

"You caught me a bit off guard too, especially when I saw... us together." He gives me one of those kinds of shy smiles, one side of his mouth lifting exposing a dimple in his cheek. It's so damn genuine it takes my breath away.

"It's one of the most incredible things I've ever seen, and I'm looking forward to living it."

I am too, but I don't say it out loud. Bael and I aren't there yet.

Heat zips through my stomach and down to my toes. After a night of toe-curling sex with *two* hot men, it should be the furthest thing from my mind. That's obviously not the case. His smile turns more charming as his nostrils flare. Bael knows it too.

"When do you want to blood bond?" I ask, thinking about way more than sucking on his finger.

"Whenever you're ready, Keri, but I suggest when it happens they keep me well away from you."

"Why?" I shiver as I ask, already knowing but wanting to hear it. My heart has been stomped on; there's no harm in a stunning man wanting to get in my pants.

"Because I want you too much."

My lips part and I lick my suddenly dry lips. He's right. We do need to be kept apart, left with him I might very well tackle fuck him and not give a damn who sees. There's anticipation strung tight between us and has been for a long while now. When it finally coalesces... boom.

"How about right now?" He's on his feet the second the words leave my mouth.

"I very much agree."

Ciar and Trick come strolling out of whatever bush they were eavesdropping from.

"A simple cut on your fingers will suffice. Trick will take you to Nagan's home until the bond lust passes. I'll take Keri the opposite direction," Ciar explains, standing face to face with Bael.

Bael surprises me again and says, "I know there is a history between us but I am all about Keri now. The past no longer exists, only our future as a Triad." Well, I thought he was hot before; now I think he's a damn inferno. I'm ready to leap on him without the bond.

He and Ciar hold each other's gazes for several minutes, weighing each other and doing that guy mojo thing men do. The tension gets so thick it's almost visible. Right as I open my mouth to say something, Ciar nods, and the weird stare off is over.

Both men relax, they've apparently reached some kind of temporary agreement.

It's totally hot.

Ciar looks at me then, smiling. He knows exactly what I'm thinking. *Me and him at once, eh Monster Girl?* he asks in my mind.

*If Puca boy doesn't do it, I will.* Trick pipes in. I laugh out loud, and Bael raises an eyebrow.

"She was picturing us fucking her," Ciar supplies in an attempt to tease me. I blush, sure, but not only because I'm a little embarrassed. It's still hot.

Ciar laughs as Bael says, "I'm okay with that."

Bael turns and kneels in front of me. A knife, gleaming silver in the dim morning light, appears in his hand, and he holds it out to me hilt first. As I pull it from his grasp, he lightly grips the blade letting it cut into his finger. While holding his gaze, I slice the tip of mine, and in sync we each hold out a bleeding digit.

His lips wrap around my finger at the same time I lick his. The bond hits me like a physical blow, taking me to my knees in front of him. The intensity climbs and climbs, making our magic visible. Even Ciar and Trick feel the backlash of it, stepping closer to us instinctively.

This is way more potent than before.

My magic spins above me and pulls in all three of theirs; combined, they create a vortex that lifts higher into the sky, growing and thundering like a growling spring storm. With a flash, the vortex reaches its pinnacle and explodes outwards, and I feel the magic inside of me grow and stretch.

"Holy fuck," Trick mutters, but I can't look away. My attention is all on Bael. He's smiling at me like a man who sees something he wants and by the gods do I want him. Now.

Firm but gentle hands pull me away from him as Trick grabs the taller Fae and takes him in the opposite direction.

"I need her," Bael protests, fighting against Trick's hold.

"You chose well, Keri," Ciar whispers in my ear as he lifts me into his arms. The fog of lust falls over me entirely, and I'm lost to coherent thought.

AFTER SEVERAL HOURS I CAN—MOSTLY—THINK coherently again. For the longest time, it was touch and go. I'd get moments of clarity or at least moments I remember. I begged Ciar to take me to Bael. I threatened, I cried, and eventually, I lay in his lap and sobbed. The strength of that bond finalizing the Triad is ridiculous.

Yet a small part of me feels like I betrayed Rime, which is stupid. He was the one off sticking his dick in other people. Oh, and betraying me to Daya. But even knowing those things it's bittersweet. I genuinely loved him and yet it fades a little more every day. I've never been one to wallow too long in heartbreak; it doesn't do anything but make it worse.

Always moving forward is my motto. It has to be. I don't live in a world where I can take a time out and get my head together or my aura aligned or whatever stupid title you want to put on it. My world is mostly do or die, and I'd rather not die.

That doesn't mean I don't care what happens to him. It just means that I'm done trying to love him. And in some ways I'm a practical soul. I need a Triad, and Bael was cheated his place in it. In all honesty, he's the one I should feel sorry for even if he freaked me out in the beginning. He helped me during the trial, he's been a quiet—sometimes annoying—presence but always consistent.

And so damn patient. He didn't give up on me even though I was unsure of having anything to do with him. But Rime, he cut ties the first chance he got. Says a lot about how dumb I am when it comes to picking boyfriends. Well—I look at Ciar—not so dumb most of the time.

He smiles down on me, privy to my thoughts, and rubs my cheek.

"It's okay you loved him, or even still do. Bael and Trick aren't going to rush you into anything, Keri. Trick is great, and you're all he thinks about even when the bond was broken. Bael is a dickweed but even he thought about you nonstop without a bond. Those are genuine feelings, don't second guess everything because of Rime. You didn't make a mistake loving him. He made a mistake *not* loving you enough."

He catches the tear that slips out with his thumb and leans down to kiss me softly.

"You feel that thrum between all four of us now?" Ciar asks. I nod, unable to remotely deny its existence. It's like a live wire in my chest, pulsing with my heart. The presence of it is a little unnerving and awesome at the same time. As much as it freaks me out, I don't want it to ever go away.

"That's a *real* Triad bond. I can't believe I didn't realize how much ours was lacking. In that, I failed you." He didn't, but it doesn't hurt to let him take the blame once in a while, keeps him humble.

He gives me a mock dirty look and does the ultimate bad. He tickles me. Giggling, I try to roll away from him and end up face first on the ground with grass and dirt in my mouth. His laughter echoes above me, and he doesn't even have the decency to stop laughing when he helps me up.

"You know, I didn't give you shit for licking your own butt," I say, walking back towards the village. I'm hungry, and I smell food. It's already midday, and I haven't eaten since the night before. I've got a magic hangover to top hangovers and can't get the taste of dirt out of my mouth.

"Hey, it was one time!" Ciar protests easily catching up with me.

"Sure it was," I snark, refusing to look at him. If I do, I'll laugh, and my pretend mad moment will be over with. "You licked your balls an awful lot for someone who just did it one time. The Fairies used to watch you do it, and they had bets on how long it lasted." I even won a time or two. Who knew someone could lick their own balls for an hour?

Bael and Trick are once again waiting for us at the fire. Bael looks as rough as I feel, and his eyes track me all the way to the fire. Both of them have plates of food, breakfast if the smell is any indication. Trick learned early on that I have a weakness for bacon. When I walk up to him he hands me a plate that he had tucked somewhere beside him. I thump down on one of the benches and start to eat.

As a piece of bacon is halfway to my mouth, Trick stands, talks about it being hot, and takes his shirt off. The bacon misses my mouth entirely and stabs my cheek.

"What did Mada have to say?" Ciar asks, amusement lacing his voice.

"She gave me two pieces of bark and told me to plant them where I'm the most vulnerable." Trick catches my eye and winks at me, flexing as he leans back, exposing all of that wonderfully smooth tattooed skin.

Damn good looking men distracting me from bacon and turning me into a horny teenager.

"That's unusual, she must be worried—" Ciar's words cut off when the forest goes silent, and a push against the wards brings everyone awake and to the common area. Mada strolls in last and stares at a place directly in front of Ciar.

A Fairy dressed in the finest clothing I've ever seen appears out of thin air. His form wavers as he looks at Ciar and unrolls a scroll.

"The first trial is about to begin. You may journey with

your Triad and rely on their assistance for this trial. 'The Lord of Death must give the gift of life,'" he announces, his voice booming unnaturally. His lavender eyes crinkle at the corners as he smiles at Ciar and disappears.

Ciar grimaces and looks at me and says, "So it begins." His quest to get his crown is a reality. Not like we needed more shit heaped on our heads or anything.

"Apparently. How in the hell do we find out who you're supposed to give life to?" I ask. As far as I know, Ciar doesn't have that kind of magic.

"Knowing Faerie, it's an overly complicated problem with a simple solution," he answers.

I look at where the messenger of Faerie—because who else can it be—and see a spattering of flower petals. That's odd, so I file it away in my brain for later.

"It's a necessary evil. When I get the crown, I can stand equal with Daya," Ciar muses, sitting his plate of food aside. "We'll need to cut our visit short. First, we have to find your wayward Familiars. They're wandering around in the forest."

"Look for the slowest, dumbest food animal here, and you'll find them. Zag is a lazy hunter," I say, cramming the last few pieces of now cold bacon in my mouth.

"I can hunt just fine, Keri. It's the worm that pounces on anything that looks edible. He tried to eat a Minotaur, and we've been their 'guests' all night. Thanks for worrying and coming to rescue us," Zag says, his sarcasm in full swing.

"But you did escape, since you're here," I tease him, hiding the fact that I really was a little worried when I Ciar said they were gone all night. Fluffy slithers into the clearing and heads straight for my lap, landing hard enough that we flip back over the bench, and I lay there with the fat, happy slob laying on me. "Fluffy, move buddy—you're squishing my breakfast out."

"Which hole?" Zag asks deadpan.

"Going to be your hole in a minute dragon," I threaten.

"This is what you signed up for, Bael. Happy?" Ciar teases, and I try to blend in with the dirt. At least I'm not eating it this time. Then again, my shirt is wet because I'm pretty sure my lovely familiar drooled all over me.

"Fluffy, Zag said he has a snack for you," I say, patting my squishy companion who's squishing me. His weight is instantly gone, and the angry squawk of Zag trying to get away from the same treatment is enough to make me lay there and laugh for a minute before sitting up. I'm not the only one, and everyone is laughing, even Bael.

These moments are why I fight so hard. They're also the ones I hold onto so hard. Take any happy you can get when you get it and never let it go.

"Are you going to get off your ass and help us pack, or are you going to sit there in that puddle of congealing drool?" Ciar asks, looking down at me. In reaction, I jump to my feet and chase him around the clearing. When I finally catch him, after Trick trips him, I rub my shirt all over him, and when he makes a sound that resembles a gag I laugh even harder.

"They say you should share everything in your relationships!" I yell, holding onto him like a randy octopus. "This is me sharing and caring!"

Suddenly I have an armful of fur, and I swear to the gods as he slips out of my arms; he squeaks out a fart. Only dog farts smell that horrendous; gagging I give up the chase.

"That was dirty, Ciar! Dog farts should be illegal!"

The laughter following that proclamation is enough to make me laugh/gag again and feel satisfied when he stops at the edge of the clearing and gives me a look of death.

*Who's playing dirty now, Monster Girl?* I did, and I have no shame about it.

*Oh, I'll show you dirty later. I'll cover you in my drool.*
*That I can get behind.*

*But you have to promise me one thing.*
*Anything.*
*No licking your butthole beforehand.*

His laughter fills my head, and I climb to my feet. Another moment to keep close to my heart as the world tries to rip it to shreds. This is my armor. Happiness.

## CHAPTER 11

## A WORM IN MY PIE

F inally home, we manage to get everything unloaded out of the wagon, Gertie shows up outside and looks at me with her arms crossed and her foot tapping, while hovering six feet in the air. Not sure what I did wrong in her eyes, but I'm sure it's legitimate. Gertie has the patience of a saint unless you're messing up the house.

"Your clothes look like you took a dust bath with some grass thrown in. What explanation do you have for yourself?" she demands a frown on her face and a twinkle in her eye, but before I can stutter out an answer, her small but strong as hell arms wrap around my neck in a hug.

"Hi, Gertie," I say with a chuckle.

"I wanted to thank you for bringing Kip with you. A Brownie without a family is in constant danger; you helped him and us without thought to yourself," she whispers into my hair, sounding a little choked up. Touched, I hug her back and pretend like I don't know that she's crying.

"He's the reason I was able to get out of there."

"That's not the way he tells it. Come inside. I made pie," she says releasing me and floating in the front door where our luggage starts to follow her like a herd of sheep. Brownie magic is so cool.

Speaking of magic. "We need to see if I have any new tricks since we're a full Triad again," I say to no one in particular. All three of the guys are standing behind me. Feeling eyes on my butt, I smile and give it an extra wiggle as I walk towards the door. The fact that I trip over the top step and stumble unsexily into the front door doesn't change the fact that they all still looked at my ass.

The smell of warm apple pie and home fills my senses as I pull together the strings of my dignity. Patting Fluffy, who is halfway up the wall, leaning on it and looking through the kitchen door eagerly, I laugh at the excited vibrations I can feel under my palm. We have to beat the worm to the pie if we hope to get any. Pushing him hard enough to make him slide down the wall, I break into a run towards the kitchen.

I love Gertie's pies, and I'll be damned if anyone but me is getting the first piece.

When I skid into the kitchen and automatically look at the kitchen island where she leaves the pies to cool, I make a face. Zag is sitting there with his tail curled around the half-empty pie pan, licking crumbs off his claws with a look of pure triumph on his face.

That dirty little lizard.

"The early bird gets the worm," he snarks just as Fluffy launches himself at the pie and the unfortunate dragon who is too busy preening and not paying attention. There's a loud crash, a miniature roar, and the crashing of glass and metal as everything on the island, including the Dragon, go flying from Fluffy's significant weight barrelling into everything.

When the noise settles, and the laughter quiets down enough, I hear Zag cussing up a storm from the floor. "If I wouldn't break the house, I'd grow to my normal size and eat you, you giant pain in the ass," he mutters.

Gertie, my hero for the day, says, "And here is the second pie. I expected some type of disaster to unfold because of these two." I cheer and snag the pie from where it hovers in midair and grab a fork out of the drawer.

I settle myself at the table and watch Zag crawl around the edge of the counter to glare at me. When Trick tries to snag a bite of pie, I growl at him and hold the pan close to me like a babe. This is *my* pie. He holds up his hands in mock surrender and slowly backs away. Ciar and Bael watch me with amusement, and Zag grumbles about not getting to eat the rest of the pie he pirated.

Poof Fluffy chitters and looks at me in hope.

Who can resist a face like that?

When I give him the three-quarters of the pie I didn't eat, Zag looks at me accusingly, and even the guys give me a look of disgust. "What? He's cuter than the rest of you."

"*He's* cuter than the rest of us?" Trick asks a teasing light in his eyes, right before he turns into a replica of Fluffy.

Curling my lip, I say, "Yeah, it's just not the same." Somehow he pulls off a sad face with whatever Fluffy has that's considered lips.

Shifting back into himself, he says, "It's shower time for me and a few hours of sleep." Leaning down he kisses me rather soundly, licking his lips as he heads upstairs.

"I'm going to shower and then plant this piece of bark in the yard. Then I'm going to head down to the butcher shop and talk to Bert. Hopefully, I still have a job."

"Why do you need a job? Ciar and I are both wealthy and have more than enough to support our household," Bael says sounding exactly like the prince he technically is.

"Boredom," I answer, smiling to distract him from the same argument that Ciar made when I said I wanted a job.

Bael looks at Ciar, who's looking at him and says, "Ah." More of that guy mojo crap.

"I need to get a few things settled with my estate and father, and then I'll return," Bael says, and then he leaves the kitchen.

Ciar looks at me and shrugs, and then he too leaves.

There's no way that all three of them are okay with me walking to the shop by myself. All of them had a convenient excuse to disappear at the same time. Licking the fork, since I have no more pie, I nudge Fluffy off my numb foot and head upstairs to the master bedroom. I'll wait until the guys are done washing up before I hop in. Hot water isn't infinite, and neither is water pressure. I don't want to stand under a trickle and feel like I'm a wilted plant having lukewarm water dumped on me.

Piddling around the room, I pick out some clothes, avoid looking in the mirror—I have a few new scars now, and some bruises still leftover—and attempt to kill time until at least one of them is finished. Ciar is the first one, and he strolls out of the steamy bathroom, wearing nothing but a smile with an invitation in it.

Faerie, I'm so tempted. But I'm also determined to speak with Bert. He's gotten nothing but silence from my end since everything happened. I'm a terrible employee.

Avoiding Ciar's grab for me, I duck, slap him on his bare ass, and dart into the bathroom. When I turn on the water and discover way more pressure than I expected I jump in without checking the temperature because sometimes, I'm just that dumb. Cold water rains down on me with the strength of a waterfall, and because I'm already committed, with a lot of cursing, I finish my shower despite my chattering teeth.

They could've at least saved me warm water.

After my cold—exhilarating Zag corrected me while I cussed every time I had to rinse a body part—I plant the piece of bark in the front yard and gawk with my mouth open as this ward trickles upwards to join the dome of our wards to strengthen them. No one is getting through those, not even Daya. The instant relief I feel almost makes me sit on the porch and cry. Being afraid of someone all the time isn't a fun loop to be stuck in, and I'm definitely afraid of him.

Fear is a perfectly healthy response to a megalomaniac with psychotic tendencies.

When I spin around to avoid giving in and having a mini-breakdown, I discover Zag perched on the gate post with Fluffy posed like a cobra waiting to strike. Apparently, I'm not going anywhere without them. Not that I mind, I haven't gotten to spend a lot of time with my Familiars, and this will give us a chance to have some genuine bonding time without the guys. Plus, it gives me a bonafide excuse to stop at the Fairy bakery in town.

And time to think.

Something I take advantage of as we walk towards the butcher shop It's hard to do that when I'm surrounded by all of those—my brain kind of goes into duh mode when I picture shirtless Ciar. Yeah, *those*. It's incredible how their nearness in certain circumstances turns me into a horny idiot.

Then there's Bael. Who looks hot with his shirt off too. I've not even touched him yet, and I know what he looks like naked, and he's all abs and long legs. Unfortunately, I have no idea how to act with him. I mean, I want to be affectionate, that's the type of person I am. But when it comes to going further thinking of snowflake stops me—or at least slows me down dramatically.

Every day that passes, I love Rime a little less, but I still love him. And the hurt that I try to avoid is still there like a splinter under my fingernail. Except this one is in my heart. I can't move forward with Bael, maybe not even with Trick until I deal with the mess of Rime.

After a few hours of fantastic sex with Trick, yeah—I love him. But it's that kind of love you feel in the beginning before it deepens. The one full of that first sexual flush and honeymoon fever. To be fair to him, I am heading towards the deeper stuff. How can I not? He goes out of his way to be good to me. However, I think I'm a bit gun shy.

What if all of this is the magic of the bond tricking me again? Or should I say being tricked? Isn't that what Rime did? He used some mojo from Daya and slipped into the bond without me sensing he wasn't meant for it. I'm fully aware that a bond can be hijacked and that people do it all the time, and their Center doesn't even realize it, but I was hyperfocused on it. I should've caught it.

It does explain the weird reluctance I had about it. Something inside of me knew something was wrong. Maybe that's why the magic showed me that Bael's fate was to get naked with me?

I shake my head and try to rattle loose the thoughts that won't go away.

Rime doesn't love me the right way. It's enough to activate his curse but not enough to break it. And even with his betrayal, it makes me sad. Deep down, Rime is a nice guy. Kind of dumb sometimes, and he needs to be told what to do like a child more often than I liked, but I saw his kindness. Felt it.

Bael is the complete opposite in most ways. He's older—not that I know exactly how old he is—he's powerful. He's manipulative, arrogant and pampered to the point I'll probably tease him in the future about someone else wiping his ass for him with golden toilet paper. Yet, he's the genuine one out of the two. I trust Bael not to hurt me.

I can't trust Rime like that anymore.

I can't have him in my life anymore, either.

Fairyfarts, how was I so fooled?

"Why are you pulling your hair like that?" Zag asks, alighting on my shoulder and poking me in the cheek with a sharp claw. I release the death grip I have on the sides of my hair and clear my throat.

"Thinking about Rime."

"Ah, that mess. I'm truly sorry you had to go through that."

"I can honestly say I'll get over it and mean it this time, but that doesn't make it easier to deal with now. Not with everything else going on."

"You're bonding well with Trick," he states, nuzzling my cheek.

"Yeah, he's a big sweetie, to be honest. Kind of like the filling in a nuget. Ciar is the smooth, crisp chocolate on the outside, Trick is the gooey center, and Bael is the crunchy almonds inside." I make a noise in my throat that's part laugh and part snort. It's an apt description and makes me crave chocolate to boot.

"I know you're hesitant, and in most circumstances I would never rush you considering what happened, but," there's always a but, "the blood bond won't be enough to concrete this type of Triad in place. Yours is an all-in kind of bond. Body, heart and soul."

"I'm aware, but I can't make my heart do whatever I want it to do, Zag. It has its own mind, and I'm usually just along for the ride." Saying that doesn't mean there isn't room for more in my heart, it just means that I'm sore from getting reamed. Hard. Without any foreplay even.

"Sometimes, the heart is a foolish organ, but it's also one that is capable of healing more than any other and growing to make room for many others as well." I flick the end of his tail.

"How many relationships have you had, Oh, Great One?"

"Well, uh—that has nothing to do with yours!" he protests.

"It's sound advice, but I still have to tease you about your virgin status." He sputters and grumbles, burying himself in my hair but not protesting. Faerie save us, he's a virgin?! "Aww, I'm sorry, Zag, I didn't know," I say, mostly meaning it. That doesn't stop me from having a giggle about it.

I'm not even sure how dragons deal with that stuff. They think and act like people, so I imagine they do the whole one night stand thing like anyone else unless it's the soulmate or bust stuff. Entirely possible, could be why there's not that many dragons floating around.

Forcing my thoughts to sober, I say, "I'll do what I need to do, but the rest of the stuff will come when it comes. I can't force myself to love someone."

"Are you attracted to Bael?" Zag asks, pretending like I wasn't teasing him about his lack of experience in the dragon-sex department.

"Duh, have you looked at him?"

"I think you and I have extremely different tastes in part-ners," he answers, his voice thick with sarcasm.

"Unless female dragons have a six-pack and a butt you can bounce coins off of, probably," I joke.

"I have seen some dragon females with lovely wingspans," he says, completely serious.

"Does that make you a boobs guy? Cos, I mean, they connect somehow to the boobs."

Fluffy makes a noise that resembles a phlegmy laugh, which makes me laugh. A worm understood a boob joke.

"That's something I love about you," Zag says, poking his head out of my hair to nuzzle my cheek again. I admit I'm completely charmed. He rarely says such sentimental things quite so baldly.

"What's that?"

"Your sense of humor and ability to laugh, no matter what. It makes you incredibly special on top of the hundreds of things that already make you special. I'm thankful that fate chose me to be your Familiar." I'm so shocked. I stop walking and look at him. He gives me the equivalent of a Dragon smile and curls his head around my neck to take a nap. He would dip out after saying something so profound.

Fluffy chitters and runs ahead of me when the butcher shop comes into view. Picking up my pace, I catch up to him and grab the door before he rips it off in his haste to get inside. Bert has a habit of feeding both of them, and Fluffy is especially spoiled because of it.

Apprehension and guilt make me hesitate in the threshold. I almost called Bert to avoid speaking with him face to face, but in most things, I'm not a coward, and there's always a chance he'll forgive me and let me keep my job. I happen to like it here.

"Don't dawdle, come in and have some lunch," comes the familiar voice from behind the counter. With an apologetic smile on my face, I shut the door and head around the counter, greeted by him operating the stove with his apron on. He looks over his shoulder at me and flips the steak that's sizzling merrily and always comes out cooked perfectly.

"I hear you've had quite the adventure," he says, turning with a full plate held out towards me. I take it sheepishly and try to ignore the fact that my mouth is watering. No one can cook steaks like Bert. Something Gertie can never find out about.

"Something like that," I answer around a mouthful of partially chewed steak.

"I also hear you need a Patron."

"Where'd you hear that from?" I ask, swallowing and chugging some water from the sweating cup that he hands me. His ever-present calm smile is in place, and of course I spill my guts.

I tell him about Daya kidnapping me and crying while still eating the food—it's too good to let get cold—I explain what happened at Daya's. My escape and Bis taking me home, and then I move onto Rime. I don't know why I tell everything, even things I haven't wanted to think on, but I do until the entire awful story has wrung me out, and I go through three tissues just to get the snot out of my nose.

"It will get better," he says, patting my back. "I can't fix what has already happened, but I can help with one of your current problems. I'll be your Patron, and I'll file the paperwork this afternoon." I'm so shocked by his statement that my mouth opens and closes several times before I get any words out.

"Really?"

"Yes, really. I might have retired, but I carry enough clout in our world to serve as your Patron. However, keep in mind that when it comes to your safety and happiness that role will give me the go ahead to meddle in some circumstances." I'm so excited about him being my Patron and saving me the hassle and potential awfulness.

Jumping to my feet, I hug him, and when he hugs me back he lifts me into his arms and reminds me for that few seconds of Nagan. It looks like I have more than one *good* dad-like person in my life now. He pats my back and sets me on my feet.

Turning, he deftly cuts a hunk of roast and without looking, tosses it over his shoulder to Fluffy. He snaps it out of the air and gobbles it down greedily.

"You lot spoil him, what are you going to do when he moves on to larger prey?" Zag asks snootily.

Bert turns and raises an eyebrow at him. With a knowing

smile on his face, he tosses Zag a piece of meat that he greedily snatches out of the air.

"At that point, you two can be hunting buddies since you know where all the good cows are," Bert replies.

"They're easy on my stomach," Zag defends, trying to look more aloof than he is.

"Sure they are," I tease. "I doubt they even look up from chewing grass when you snag them." Zag sticks his tongue out at me but doesn't argue.

"Now, about work. My first recommendation as your Patron is for you to take time off until things have settled. I can't have my favorite employee stressed and unable to enjoy their job." I'm his only employee, but I don't say that out loud. "Trying to juggle a new Triad member, the heartbreak from an old one, a High-Priest of Donn who's trying to kidnap you... is too much for anyone to handle. Even you, Keri. Take time off and I expect you to return to work refreshed and happy."

When it says it that way, it's a lot more than I realized.

Still, taking on the responsibility of being my Patron isn't easy. "Bert, are you sure about being my Patron? You'll have to deal with all of the bullshit going on in my life, and I don't want you hurt," I protest, finally finding the ability to speak coherently. I'm incredibly relieved and excited that he's offered, but I also don't want to drag him into the absolute mess of my life because of his kindness.

"I've had a boring retirement, and I think it's time to spice it up," he teases and subtly pushes me towards the door while shoving two brown bags full of goodies into my hands. "One bag is for your Familiars, the other for you." He opens the door and hurries me, Zag and Fluffy, out of it. "I'll come visit soon." Then he shuts the door and turns the sign to closed.

What the hell just happened?

"That was interesting," Zag muses, flying up to my shoulder to nose around the top of the paper bags.

"Do you know something I don't?"

"Always," he says, sticking his nose in the top of one bag. I smack it, and his nose. "Ow! Was that necessary?"

"Yes."

Blowing shadows into my hair, he harrumphs and digs around like a cat and settles himself as close to the bags as possible without actually being in them. "You have no idea who he is, do you?"

"He's Bert the butcher."

"There are days I worry about your mind," he mutters and then turns to look me in the eyes. "Your new Patron is the king of the Bloodcaps."

"Oh. Shit."

"Yes, one of the few remaining Unseelie kings. I suspected but didn't know for sure until he said he would be your Patron, and his crown briefly appeared on his head, but you were too busy blowing your nose to notice."

Digesting this latest news, including the fact that because of Bert, I have one less worry looming over my head, I walk towards home.

When we pass the bakery, I pause, and then when the temptation is too much to resist, duck inside with Fluffy hot on my tail. After loading up on lots of sad-mood-food and some of my other favorites, I end up stopping at the clothing store next.

Kip needs clothes, and it gives me an excuse to look at some of their new stuff. Everyone needs a little pick-me-up outfit. After the month I've had, I might need three or four.

I end up with ten.

## CHAPTER 12
## AS SNEAKY AS FLUFFY IN A BAKERY

We end up stopping at the park, I'm fully aware that Daya could show up at any time but for the life of me, I can't get the motivation to go home. After visiting the Dark Forgetful Forest, I want to be out in the open. Not holed up in a house with three alpha males who are all on overprotective mode. Leaning down, I dig a small hole in the soft soil with my hand and plant the second piece of bark that Mada gave me.

It's impulsive and potentially the wrong place to put it, but I like coming here, and I'd rather be safe when I do. When I cover the bark, green magic trickles out and rises into the sky to form a dome of protection over the entire park.

Smiling I watch the pigeons pecking at the ground all around us and Fluffy—who's hiding under the bench making cooing noises because he wants to snack on one—makes me feel sorry enough for him that I take a roll out of the bakery bag and toss out pieces to draw them closer to the bench.

That's the moment I notice that I'm being followed. All three of them were at least clever enough to shield themselves from the bond, but now there's a pair of bright green eyes peeking out from a bush. Ciar, obviously. The bush itself doesn't look like it belongs there either. And there's Trick.

Looking past the bush-that-isn't-a-bush, I see Bael standing behind a tree that's half his size, trying to blend in, which is made even harder because he's wearing a bright white t-shirt. Since I'm looking at them out of the corner of my eye, I don't think they've noticed that I've seen them.

Fake coughing into my hand, I hide a laugh.

"They're desperately trying to give you privacy and not upset you by being incognito," Zag says in amusement.

"They seriously suck at it," I whisper from under my hand.

A burst of feathers in front of me and the gross sounds of Fluffy crunching on the unfortunate pigeon like a cracker gives me an excuse to laugh. My thoughts move onto the quest, it's been in the back of my mind all day, but other things were precedent.

Now that one problem is taken care of, I have to move onto the next one. The Quest.

"Where do you think we need to start with the first part of the quest?" I ask Zag.

"I don't think it's a soul, that would be too easy and yet impossible at the same time. Ciar can't return a soul, and I doubt Faerie would set him up for failure."

"Then it's something specific that only *he* can bring back to life."

More feathers blow out from under the bench, and I shift my legs to keep anything from getting on them. Who knows how many he'll eat while I sit here. Fluffy is getting ready to hit another growth spurt and is guzzling as many calories as he can get in his cute, fat face. Where he's from food is scarce, and they have been known to each other. The desert isn't kind to any of its creatures.

When the epiphany hits me, I jump to my feet. "That's it!"

"What's it?" Bael calls out, only to be shushed by the other two. Turning towards them, I roll my eyes.

"I already know you three are there, come out." The Puca strolls out first, prancing like a horse who won the show, and Trick—who was the bush—straightens up and has the sense to blush when he meets my eyes. Bael is as bad as Ciar, except he's prancing on two legs.

"There's a flower called the 'Death Blossom.' It grows only in the desert, and for all sense and purposes is dead until something bleeds on it," I say excitedly. "Blood brings it to *life*."

Ciar shifts from one breath to the next and has his arms around me.

"Where do we find this flower?" Bael asks, watching me but keeping a small distance between us. Hard to believe that the man I met in the grocery store months ago is standing before me and respecting my boundaries.

"Any major desert where the worlds merged," I answer as Ciar sets me on my feet. "Do you think it's the right thing?" I ask him anxiously.

"Worth a try. Anyone up for a trip?" He says with a smile.

WE END UP PICKING THE DESERT THAT FLUFFY TAKES TO immediately. It was only a half-night trip by wagon, and miraculously I slept most of the way. I heard bits and pieces of their conversation as I dozed in and out. The atmosphere between the three of them is surprisingly light considering that Bael is still new to the mix.

The ground is rumbling like an underground thunderstorm, and there are zero signs of life except underground.

Fluffy's kind lives here and from the sounds of things, in abundance.

"Okay, Fluffers, you gotta take us a safe way to the Death Blossom," I ask my distracted familiar. He turns his bulbous head and chitters then launches himself forward.

We have to run to keep up with him, but he takes us in a sure and straight direction. Eventually his pace slows, and my legs thank him heartily as I'm bent over, my hands resting on my sore knees, trying to catch a decent breath Fluffy trumpets. I wave the guys ahead and lag behind. I'm so out of shape. I can't remember the last time I went jogging or did a sit up.

When I catch up to them, they're all standing around this ugly orange, wilted looking weed. My imagination painted it to look much different. "Are you sure this is it?" I ask.

"Fluffy seems to think so, and normally I don't trust him to lead me anywhere except to something he finds edible, but in this case, he'd be the only one who knows. We looked all over the LeyNet for pictures but found none," Zag answers.

"Well, Ciar, go stab your finger and drip on it," Trick says with an encouraging push to Ciar's shoulder. Ciar gives him a look but otherwise does as bid. He pulls his knife and cuts across the pad of his thumb. Holding it above the flower he squeezes until it drips down onto the dead plant.

We all stare at it expectantly, and after a few minutes of nothing happening, there's a group sigh of disappointment.

"Well, I guess I was wrong." My cheeks are hot, and I kind of want to throw up. The hope that has kept me going for the entire night gets sucked out of me. For once I thought I had come up with the solution. Instead, I wasted valuable time.

Damn it all.

"Wait, Keri look," Zag says, hitting me with one of his wings. Pulling myself out of my pity party, I look at the weed

—that isn't a weed anymore. As I watch it glows and fills out, unfurling it's withered leaves and petals to reach towards the night sky in vivid oranges and reds.

"You have passed the first trial," the messenger announces from behind us, causing every single one of us to react. I almost jumped out of my skin, Ciar turned into a wolf and is facing the Fairy snarling. Trick is some big monster looking thing with long claws, and Bael has swords. Two glowing red swords. Zag is almost full size and Fluffy—mid leap—turns himself to hit the ground next to the Fairy instead of landing on the small man's head.

He's definitely laughing at us with his eyes as he continues, "The second trial will require strength and perseverance. In three days at sunrise, it will begin. 'The one that hunts must instead be hunted.' You must survive a full day alive." Then he disappears again, leaving us all standing there, or in Fluffy's case laying there, staring at the empty spot where he stood.

"Fuck," Ciar barks out, standing naked and angry in front of me.

## CHAPTER 13

## DEFENSE OF THE HEART

The pounding on the front door drags me from a dreamless sleep. I roll over and find the bed empty of my two sleeping companions. Ciar is probably on a hunt, and Trick is more than likely hiding in the basement with his headphones on doing whatever it is he does on his computer. With a groan I crawl out of bed and head in the general direction of the front door.

Halfway down the stairs, the murmur of male voices stops me in my tracks. One of them is raised in anger and unwanted. Rime. While the other is calm, cold even, but calm and it belongs to Bael. And because I'm a jerk—and don't want to talk to Rime—I walk down a few more steps to be close enough to eavesdrop without being seen.

"... replaced me so soon? What happened to her 'loving' me? Considering it's her fault, I'm going to go insane and die!" Weeks ago those words would've stabbed me through the heart as painfully as a rusty knife, now even though they hurt it's more like the achy kind versus the sharp kind. His problems aren't my fault, and my head is clear enough not to take the blame for his mistakes.

"What the fuck is wrong with you? She took you into her home, into her life—loved you. And you've done nothing but betray her, lie to her and blame her for your shortcomings. You don't deserve her," Bael says so much calmer than I can ever pull off. Honestly, I think it makes me fall a little in love with him on the spot.

"She was mine first," Rime protests vehemently.

"She was never yours. You simply had the pleasure of being hers for a little while. Then you fucked that up," Bael responds as calmly as ever.

"You should be grateful I did, Fae lord," Rime says snidely.

"For being part of her life, yes, yes, I am. For her pain being the cause of it, no. Something you should be concerned about since you supposedly care about her." Good comeback, Bael. Even though having Rime this close, talking so nastily about me stings, I'm thankful that Bael answered the door instead of me.

"Hasn't she moved on rather quickly for supposedly caring about me?" What an asshole asking something like that. Even after finding out about his deal with Daya, I wanted to help him, I still do, but I have no idea how.

"What choice did you give her, Rime? You came into her life under false pretenses, you planned on working with the insane man who sired her to essentially sell her off to the highest bidder. Who tortured her, hurt her. Then you come here and try to prey upon her feelings for you because you can't hold your alcohol and feel sorry for yourself."

"I can't stay away... I love her," Rime says with more anger than love.

"Love isn't this destructive mess you want to ensnare her in."

"What could you possibly know about love?" Rime demands.

I start to walk down the stairs, but a firm but gentle grip on my elbow stops me. Trick.

"Until I met her? Nothing. But she's taught me that love means the willingness to sacrifice anything for someone. Something Keri is always willing to do for those she loves. But you, you don't have any clue what it means. All I've heard from you are unreasonable demands for her to bear the responsibility and blame for the things you've done to yourself. That isn't even close to love." Bael finishes his impassioned speech with the hollow echo of the door slamming.

Part of me hopes it hit Rime right in the face, while the rest of me feels sorry for him. Just not sorry enough to chase after him. I'm done with that part of my life, even if it still hurts.

Bael turns away from the door and starts up the stairs. He stops with one foot still raised in the air to stare at me. He had no idea I was here. I walk down the stairs separating us and wrap my arms around his waist. For several heartbeats, they are pounding in my ear. He stands there with his arms at his sides.

When he wraps them around me, smelling like mint and smoky fire, I smile and squeeze him tighter.

Tonight he's my hero and maybe in more ways than one.

"Thank you, Bael, for making it hurt less."

"Anything for you, Keri. Anything."

## CHAPTER 14
## UNCOMFORTABLY NUMB

I woke up depressed, not that I went to bed ecstatic. My mind won't let go of Rime's predicament. I shouldn't feel sorry for him, but I do. Not that it makes me want to run out and be his buddy, but his misery is tangible, and I'm not heartless enough to not *try* to do something. But I've asked everyone who knows anything about magic, and there's no solution to his problem but finding his one true love.

Rolling out of bed, I walk to the window that looks down in the backyard. The pool is sparkling in the early morning sunlight, it's chilly outside, but the fantastic thing is heated. Making up my mind, I decide to go swimming, as long as I stay in the water I won't freeze my ass off. I don't even bother with a bathing suit.

Marching downstairs, I skip the breakfast waiting on the table for me, give a cursory wave to Gertie, and Kip—who I notice is wearing his new clothes—and walk straight to the pool. Without pause I jump in and sink into the warm, soothing water. At the bottom of the deep end I wrap my arms around my knees and close my eyes.

The silence is beautiful.

When my lungs start to burn, I surface and breathe in the clean, crisp air, then back down I go. My messy thoughts begin to get organized, my aching heart starts to beat without pain. I can't waste love on someone who doesn't deserve it. He might have my sympathy, and I might want to help him, but Bael is right. What Rime feels for me isn't love. No one would do that to someone they love.

It will linger a while, but this way, I can truly let it go. Free myself from the choking sadness that I try to hide from but always finds me. The water carries my tears away so for once I can let them fall unchecked. Several more trips to the surface later, I'm worn out and lighter at the same time. When I break through the surface the final time, I look around me. I think everyone that lives with me is lined up around the pool, looking at me like I have a dick on my forehead.

"What?" I question the assembly of people.

"With the exception of Ciar, we all thought you were going to drown yourself," Zag says, dipping his foot in the water. He slides into it without a splash and swims towards me, looking like a big iguana. Doing laps around me he floats on his back and sprays water up like a fountain statue.

"Thanks for the faith in me, lizard," I ask him, sending a small wave of water towards him.

"No, you only needed to purge yourself of the sadness. You did it as a child too," Ciar says as he slides into the water too, swimming towards me like the predator he is. Smiling for the first time, I avoid him, and then with a multitude of splashing bodies everyone joins in the fun.

"You realize if you keep bringing people home, we're going to need a bigger house," Zag says, swimming close enough to talk but far enough away to avoid me.

"We can always build a new one," Bis chirps.

"Oh, my gods! A Fairy built house?" I exclaim, grabbing

onto Ciar's shoulders as he finally catches me. Treading water, we stare at each other, and the moment changes. Trick is swimming lazily behind him, smiling the charm-my-pants off smile that will get him laid in a heartbeat.

"Keri, are you naked?" Zag asks, breaking the building sexual tension. The little shit did it on purpose. I glare at the miniature Dragon, peeking up over Ciar's shoulder. Wishing for a big wave to take him under, I instead end up lifting him out of the water. He lays on his side, floating in the air, and winks at me.

Either they all have something constantly in their eyes, or I don't quite get the language of winking.

"Do you feel better?" Ciar asks, cupping my cheek with his hand.

"Yes and no."

"Why, no?"

I opt to tell him the complete truth. "I was afraid of being manipulated by magic, and that's exactly what happened. And even though I'm pushing the love, I feel for him out of my heart. I can't rid myself of the distrust of the bond."

"There's some truth that you were manipulated magically but did it not bring you three men who genuinely love you... even without the bond tied us together?" I raise an eyebrow in question, and he reads the thought in my mind. Leaning close to me he presses his nose against mine. "Even Bael."

Ciar wouldn't lie to me about such a thing, not in a million years.

"Thank you Ciar, I needed to hear that, and now I can completely let go." As Trick swims up behind me, trapping me between their warm naked bodies, Zag decides to try and be a killjoy again.

"Everybody out, they're going to do something I don't want to see."

"Shouldn't you be out chasing sleeping cows or something,

Zag?" I tease, looking away from Ciar's magnetic gaze long enough to see what the dragon—who's still floating in the air —says to that.

"I don't chase sleeping cows. I swoop them."

Laughing, I let him fall back in the water with a loud splash and with the sexual tension broken for the final time— at least in the pool—I look at Bael, who's the only one not in the water. Even Gertie and her family are swimming.

"Want to play water tag, Duke?" He holds my gaze before nodding. "Tag, you're it."

## CHAPTER 15

## ALWAYS HAVE A PLAN

After playing in the pool and running naked into the house to get dressed, with what metaphorical icicles hanging off my ass, I sit beside Bael on the couch. He's alone and looks alone. I don't like that look on him, so something has to change.

"What are you up to?" I ask, breaking his contemplative silence.

"My father wants to meet you," he answers, staring at the phone in his hand.

"Oh, yay." Meeting the king isn't one of my life goals, but I am bonded to his son, so I guess I knew in the back of my mind that it would happen one day.

"He won't harm you. My existence is too important to him." I'm sure he meant for that to sound reassuring, but in that, he failed.

"You're not saying that in a way that makes me think you think he loves you," I comment, scooting a little closer to him.

"Of course, he doesn't in the way you understand love, but I'm his only heir, and he's big on formalities."

"I'm sorry, Bael," I say, rubbing my hand on his.

He looks at me in surprise and says, "I accepted it long ago."

"A child shouldn't have to accept that ever." He doesn't say anything for several minutes. He twines his hand with mine and rubs my knuckles until they go numb. "When are we supposed to go?"

"After we take care of things here." Okay, that could take a few months. I can't say I'm sad about delaying the visit with the king.

"I'm sure I'll make quite a hit with him. He'll think I'm the biggest moron on the planet. Especially if we have dinner where they put out twenty different forks."

"You'll do fine, and I'll be right there beside you. We'll even come up with a code word for which fork to use," he teases, some of the tension leaving him.

"You've changed since I met you." And he has. He's a lot easier to make laugh, and some of the stiff arrogance has come out of him. That either shows that the arrogance— some of it anyway—is for show or I've corrupted him around to our way of thinking. It could even be both, but I'm happy with the results.

I like this side of him.

"Do you want to go shopping with me?" That question is not one I expected at all.

"You realize who you're talking to? I love shopping. Especially in Fairy stores."

"You really do have an obsession with them." I shrug, we all have our flaws and obsessions. "I happen to love model wooden ships. I have an entire collection of them at the castle." What he shared with me might not seem like much to many people, but to me it's the same as him telling me some dark secret.

I don't think his father is the type to nurture hobbies like that.

"We'll have to put one together then, I've never done it, but I admit it sounds fun." And it genuinely does. I like little detailed things like that. Takes your mind off into a special relaxing place. That's probably how Bael got into it.

"Really?" He sounds so shocked that I frown at him.

"Yeah, really. Why are you so surprised?"

"The first time a woman has ever offered something like that to me."

"What do they normally offer you?" The minute the question leaves my mouth, he smiles. One of those lippy smiles that lets you know that someone's thinking dirty thoughts.

I like that smile too.

"Many things, most of which I didn't desire from them. Now if you were to make that offer... " he teases—if he's teasing. He kind of sounds serious.

"Come on, let's go shopping," I say, dragging him to his feet.

Best to do something to occupy ourselves that doesn't involve me dragging him to bed instead.

IT'S THE NIGHT BEFORE THE HUNT BEGINS, WHICH SUCKS because it's us being hunted, not some Fae who's broken Faerie law. However, you can't tell how dangerous a situation it is by the relaxed attitude that all of the guys have.

Trick is napping on the couch, while Bael is playing a video game. Ciar is sitting in the recliner with one leg carelessly thrown over the arm, clipping his fingernails. While I'm the only apparent bundle of nerves, steadily pacing a hole in the carpet behind the couch. Finally the relaxed atmosphere gets to me.

"What the fuck, guys?" I demand, stepping in front of the TV to get their full attention.

Ciar smirks, and Bael shrugs. Trick opens his eyes and then rolls over giving me his back. "I don't get it, why aren't any of you as nervous as I am?"

"Monster Girl, this isn't the first time I've been hunted," Ciar finally answers, without looking at me.

"Me either," Trick adds.

"Same," Bael tosses in.

"Technically, it's not the first time for you either," Ciar says. My anxiety drops to almost zero with that reminder. Well, shit, he has me there. I sit on the floor where I'm standing because I'll be damned if they can't at least share this time with me.

"Someone has to have a plan?" I ask them.

"Survive."

"Great plan, Ciar. How do we do that?" All three of them look at me at once. The hairs on the back of my neck stand up. It's not easy being the focus of all three of them. It reminds me of how I felt when I peed my pants the first time.

"Keri, you have three of the strongest Fae in the world sitting in your living room, and you're asking a question like that?" Zag asks, landing on the back of the couch.

"Pardon me for not being some ageless demigod," I snark. "I don't have the juice the three of you have."

"Keri, you control fate itself," Zag argues.

"Yeah, but it has a cost." Like the multitude of brands that still hurts me on my body.

Gertie pops into the living room as the wards alarm. The guys are on their feet and heading towards the front door before I can stand. Yeah, they're way more nervous than they're letting on. They all beat me outside, and in this circumstance, I'm glad.

Daya is here.

Standing outside of our wards, he smacks them, expecting them to fall before him. Instead, they push back, and he slides several feet backward.

"You dare block my entrance, daughter?" he demands when he walks back to the border of the wards.

"Yeah, looks that way," Trick responds, leaning against the railing of the porch.

"I am not speaking to you, mongrel!" Daya bites out, and his eyes go to me, standing in the doorway. "How am I not welcomed into your home?" he asks in that soft voice that gives me the chills.

"I dunno, the whole kidnapping me and torturing me thing kinda soured our relationship, Daya," I answer, crossing my arms while trying to look way more relaxed than I am. He *scares* me and always will.

"You are a worthless progeny, and I should have allowed her to slice you out of her womb like she wanted to. But I let my softer feelings interfere. That will not be the case again!" he rants, pacing back and forth in front of the ward boundary.

This is the angriest and most demonstrative I've ever seen him, and even though it's loud and threatening, the quiet version scares me more.

"Nothing to say in your defense?" he demands, stopping to point an accusing finger at me.

"I don't need to say anything. I didn't ask you to make me. I owe you nothing, High-Priest." My voice holds the pent up rage he inspires in me, and I hope he understands that afraid or not if, given the chance, I'll end him.

"I will make another child, one more grateful than you, but you will need to be destroyed first. I refuse to allow such a rebellious child to live!" he says with heat but without raising his voice again. The creepy calm Daya is back, and even as I shiver in apprehension, I manage to remain outwardly calm.

So much so that I bite out, "Good luck, *father.*" He smiles at him, and I and his entire entourage disappear in shadows.

Looking around at the guys in the sudden silence, I opt for the braver approach and says, "Who's buying?" Laughter follows me as I walk back into the house.

## CHAPTER 16
## RUN AWAY LITTLE GIRL

As the morning approaches, the clouds, a physical display of the somber mood I'm in, block out the rising sun. It'll storm here today, but hopefully not where we need to go. Wherever that will be, we all know it'll probably be some dark, dank forest out in the middle of nowhere. It wouldn't be hard if that wasn't the case. In town we could hunker down behind our wards and wait it out.

"Does anyone have a plan yet that has more than one word in it?" I ask the gathered group. Zag blows a smoke ring and Fluffy chortles. The guys all look at me and as one, shrug. "Are you serious right now?" I demand, throwing a pillow at Ciar's head. This is *his* trial. He should have some semblance of a plan, and I say as much.

"Keri, I understand you're concerned, but I'm not. I've survived much worse, and so has Trick. Bael... well, he survived court. That's a hunt in its own right." Ciar looks at Bael, who's looking at him with a frown. He's trying to decide if he was insulted or not.

Honestly, I'm not entirely sure either.

The two of them are getting along, but at some point I

127

think they'll have more than a staring contest to settle things between them. I can only hope that all they do is see who can pee further. I'd rather them not get into a physical altercation, as sexy as some people might find that I don't. It creates discord and makes me look like a bone they're fighting over. There's nothing sexy about that considering the circumstances.

But I'm fully aware it will happen eventually, their little pissing contest. I think maybe it has to happen for us to function as a proper Triad. Not that there's a good time for it, but this is the *worst* time for it.

Bael smiles and looks back down at the phone in his hand. He decided to take it as a compliment. Thank Faerie. I'm already so tense I could open a beer bottle with my butt, the last thing in the world I need is to have more tension or stress or even a possible fistfight. If that makes me weak, then so be it. I'll take knowing my limits over having a nervous breakdown any day.

The overwhelming smell of flowers engulfs us, and when I blink we're all sprawled on the ground of—as I predicted—a dark, dank forest. Ciar is the first one to his feet, dusting off his pants; he looks around him with a critical eye. One hundred percent predator. My playful, teasing man is gone, and in his place is someone that by all rights, is scarier than Daya.

Just not to me.

Trick sits cross-legged, watching Ciar in expectation. He'll follow his lead. I don't doubt that he's a tough cookie in his own right, he's a smart one too. Ciar is familiar with hunts, no matter what kind they are, he's a good lead to follow.

Bael is looking at me, and when he stands, Ciar is ignored. This could be a problem, not that he's concerned about me but that he's not following Ciar's lead. I try to communicate that with my eyes and I even twang our bond.

*Don't be a dick, Bael.* I sent to him, hoping he listens. I know by the widening of his eyes he at least heard what I said. Since the fiasco with Rime, I've kept my shields up and stronger than before, maybe it's time to relax them a bit. Being able to speak to each other telepathically is probably the smarter option considering I have no idea what will be hunting us.

I hope it won't be the Sluagh.

"It won't be," Ciar answers my unspoken thought. And he's already in my brain.

"Any idea who?" Trick asks, climbing to his feet and stretching like he's getting ready to go jogging. Maybe that's a requirement for changing shapes? Or he's doing a bit of flexing so I'll ogle him and be distracted. He catches my gaze and smirks.

Definitely the ogling. Even in a life or death situation, I can't deny how pretty he is. It demonstrates how messed up my priorities are. Or how anxious I am considering he's resorting to flexing to take my mind off it.

Even Ciar has a small smile on his face.

Men.

Ciar's smile drops, and seriousness replaces it. "If I had to guess, and I do—probably someone I've had to hunt before. There's irony there, and Faerie is all about irony." He doesn't sound too pleased with it either.

Honesty is always important in a relationship, but I half-assed wish he'd lied. Ciar has hunted some of the most dangerous, evil creatures that have ever existed, and now we're going to be hunted by them. I think Faerie likes a little sadism with her irony.

"Have faith in us, Keri," Bael states and he too stretches like he's going jogging except in his case I don't think it's to look pretty for me. The look on his face is deadly serious, and he's looking around us instead of at me. Two wicked looking swords slide into his hands.

And of course, as my brain picks through some of the awful creatures Ciar has hunted my mother pops into my head. The Wild Hunt hunted my mother, is it possible that she will be hunting us in return? Ciar looks at me in alarm, not because he's afraid of her—he killed her after all—but because I am. All of the training and my magic is useless when it comes to the memories tainted by terror of my mother.

I'll freeze, I know I will, and that concerns me. This isn't just about me. I look at the people I love—well, mostly people—and the thought of my potential cowardice is almost enough to make me cry.

*You can do this, Keri. Even if they send three of her, you're stronger than that bitch ever was.* Ciar reassures me, and amazingly it works. Mostly. Enough that the breaths that were threatening to freeze in my chest and send me to the ground, ease in and out of me once again.

When did I become such a fucking pussy?

The answer is Daya.

Why is it that I was stuck with two psychotic parents who want me dead?

"You suffered extreme trauma from both of them, Keri. Some of which are still fresh in your mind and body. But I haven't seen you let something like that beat you yet," Ciar says, crossing to me and touching my cheek with his fingertips. "Suck it up, Monster Girl you're stronger than this. Now act that way." He smiles to soften the blow, but they're still words I need to hear, no matter how harsh they sound.

It doesn't mean I have to smile and say thank you.

There's a loud crash to our right, and then the howling starts. We're surrounded by a howl I hoped to never hear in my life.

"Trolls," all three of the guys say at once.

Oh shit.

Zag leaps upwards and is immediately repelled and knocked back to the ground. Great, they're cutting off that escape route. Fluffy does his mini-roar and takes off into the forest. I appreciate his heart, but he can't take on a Troll by himself! Zag—his full-sized self—follows me as I run after Fluffy. Trick calls after me, but I wave over my shoulders.

Sure, I'm having some anxiety issues, but I'm still capable of taking care of myself. Standing around biting my nails with dread filling my stomach is not how I usually do things. If I stay that way, Daya and my mother win. I can't have that. Besides, I know damn well all three of them are following behind the Dragon crashing through the trees like a runaway wagon.

"Zag, why didn't you go back to pocket size?" I ask, fighting through dense brush to try and keep up with Fluffy. The fat worm is moving like he's walking on air, I had no idea he could move that way.

"If I do, I won't have full access to my magic, and given that our enemies are the size of houses, I'd rather be safe than sorry." He sounds a little out of breath and for some stupid reason it strikes me as funny. Laughing, I keep moving forward.

Unfortunately, not only towards Fluffy.

There's a loud cry, possibly from a girl Troll and Fluffy roars again. Except for this time he doesn't sound quite so small. As I tear into the clearing, skidding to a stop I grab a tree to catch my balance as my mouth falls open in shock. Fluffy is no longer a baby Corpse Worm. Fluffy is as big as the Troll he has wrapped in his many legs, munching on their—her, but with Trolls it's hard to tell—shoulder like a piece of beef jerky.

"Uh, does he shrink like you do Zag?" I ask the dragon

who has his giant head hovering over my shoulder with his mouth gaping open in shock.

"I fucking hope so!" he answers, closing his mouth to watch the battle before us. The guys bring up the rear with Ciar in his canine form and Trick, a white twin. That's interesting and something I'll comment on later. Bael slips silently in between them, the swords pointing at the ground with what looks like blood dripping off them.

"Uh, why is there blood on your swords?" I ask, looking at the three of them in a new light.

"There were some obstacles," he answers, his gaze locked on the fighting giants in front of us.

"How many more do you think there are?" I ask, pointing at the manly female Troll that's steadily losing to the newly giant worm.

"Four of them. They were hunted for killing and eating humans. They took out two villages before we caught them, and it wasn't an easy takedown," Ciar says, changing into his human form.

I almost don't look at him naked. Almost.

"Shouldn't they be ghosts or something?" Trick asks, back to his usual self with his clothes on. We all look at him. "Since they're dead and all?"

"They're still dead, and if you look at her wounds there's no blood. These are imitations of the real thing but still dangerous," Ciar answers calmly, tapping his chin with a finger. He always does that when he's thinking hard about something.

"What did you run into in the forest?" I must've run right by it. I don't recall seeing anything, not that I was looking anywhere but in front of me. I figured the big Dragon walking behind me, and three Fae men was enough to keep everything else at bay.

I wasn't wrong.

"Some Siren's and another something or another," Trick answers evasively.

"There was a Graywalker, wasn't there?" I demand. He shrugs and looks everywhere but me. "It wasn't my mom, was it?" He shakes his head and finally looks at me.

"No, but there was a resemblance," he says honestly.

Graywalkers are few and far between, which means that they're probably all related. Not that I care, but I can see why he's reluctant to say anything about it. This is my fault, him treating me like a piece of glass, Ciar is right.

I hate it when he's right.

"You killed the bitch, ya?" He nods, and I turn back to Fluffy. The Troll is down on the ground, unmoving, and he's gnawing on her arm, and as gross as it is, he looks so damn happy doing it. "Fluffy, you can have lunch later!" I yell, distracting him from moving onto grosser parts.

He warbles in disappointment but turns back towards us, shaking the ground when he lands on his feet. When he moves though, he's silent as death. Something that large moving shouldn't move so quietly, I don't care if I adore him or not. He weaves around trees and the large scars they put in the earth during their battle with ease as he crosses to me.

Leaning down, he puts his multi-eyed face close to mine and coos. His breath is foul, but I still lean forward and kiss his nose. My Fluffy is all grown up now.

"I think it's safe to say the Trolls will be dealt with. We'll need to deal with everything else," I comment, tickling him under his chin. His eyes roll back in his head, and he sways slightly side to side. "Okay, go kick their asses and try not to eat too much of them. I have no way of brushing your teeth." I smile as he warbles again and rears up. Turning he dives into the ground, that shudders beneath our feet, and leaves nothing behind but a large hole.

"That's completely unexpected," Trick says, shaking his head as he stares at the hole Fluffy made.

"They all have to grow up sometime," I tease. "When are you three going to do it?" For my comedic effort, I get three sets of dirty looks. "What? It's a fair question." Turning I head back into the woods. Standing around isn't going to help our cause. Unmoving targets get caught.

*I see you paid attention to some things I taught you.* Ciar snarks.

*I know which type of moss to wipe my ass with, too, if that helps you feel like a better teacher.*

*Good to see the real Keri is back with us.*

Yeah, yeah, it is.

## CHAPTER 17
## CLEANING HOUSE, FAERIE STYLE

Four Trolls, seven Dryads, and four Kelpies later we're all laid out in the same clearing, exhausted. Even Fluffy, who is curled around us like a wagon caravan is snoring because he's exhausted. I'm covered in dead thing gook, hungry and ready to pass out. At this point I'm not even sure I can get up off the ground. I was so determined to keep up with the guys I might have overdone it.

Zag lets out a loud snore and moves in his sleep. Patting him, I try to push his wing off my face to no avail. He's back to pocket-size but he's also sleeping nearly on my head.

Turning my head so I can not breathe in Dragon butt, my eyes fall on Ciar, leaning against a tree. He is covered in gore and dirt. Ciar fights with a ferocity that I've never seen the equal of. He tears through his opponents with precisely controlled violence and is beautiful to watch fight. Not once did he use any weapons besides his claws and body. Out of all of the training he's ever done with me, this is the first time I've seen him fight in such a way.

I knew he was a badass, but this was something else entirely.

Trick is leaning against the tree next to Ciar, his head down in weariness. He too looks worse for wear. And he also surprised me. Trick is a dirty fighter; he changes forms and sneaks up on his opponents. They're dead before they hit the ground, and he's moving onto the next one. His body is any weapon he chooses it to be, and even though he doesn't fight with the same joy that Ciar does, he fights to win.

Trick isn't just the goofy, flirty one.

Of course, my eyes move onto Bael, who's sitting on a stump, cleaning one of his swords. Bael is eloquence incarnate. With his blades he's a whirling, dancing killer. Each stroke of his blade is deadly and powerful. Magic lights them up like lanterns and burns through his enemies with ease. Not once did the arrogant man break a sweat, and although he's as dirty as the rest of is, he's wearing it like a fashion statement. No matter where he goes in his life or who he's with, he'll always be a prince. One who has killed before and has no problem doing it again when necessary.

Bael is a killer like Ciar is. I saw the joy on his face.

"If you'd listened when I told you to take out the Dryad leader, we'd have dropped them faster," Ciar says, breaking the heavy silence. Uh-oh.

When Ciar called out the order as the Dryads rushed us, Bael completely ignored him, focusing on a Kelpie instead. To be fair, he killed it, but it also left the Dryads fighting strong. I can't disagree with Ciar being upset by it.

And if they have it out now, I'll watch from my lumpy, wet spot on the ground. Morning is lighting the sky, and soon the Trial will be over, a full day has passed, and I feel every minute of it if they want to punch each other to assuage their egos, more power to them. It's bound to happen sooner or later anyhow, and this way, they can't break the house.

"You're not my lord and master, Ciar. I do what I wish," Bael finally answers.

"Not when it goes against the team as a whole, *Fae Lord*. You put all of us in danger because of your fucking ego. Don't make me put it in check," Ciar says it softly, without menace, but because I know him so well, I hear the promise of violence underneath it.

Oh, boy. He's pissed.

In a roundabout way, I feel sorry for Bael, but in some ways not so much. Car is the Pinnacle for a reason. He has age and experience on the man. Unless Ciar is demanding something ridiculous or steering us into a bad place, Bael should—in the least—consider Ciar's opinion. Circumventing him and being obstinate for the hell of it doesn't help us become a more cohesive unit. If anything, it makes us less so.

"I dare you to try," Bael remarks, his voice snidely condescending. Well, there went the small hope he would agree to work with him.

Using what little energy I have left, I roll away from them towards Fluffy's protective bulk, taking the sleeping Dragon with me—who sputters awake and starts complaining.

"Ciar and Bael are about to have their pissing contest, I suggest you shut up," I whisper to him.

"Oh—oh!" The foggy-headed Dragon says, coming to his feet to blatantly watch. Of course I prop myself up enough to see too. I'm not happy it's happening, but I'm not about to miss this either. It's not that I'm rooting for either one of them, a little humility wouldn't hurt either, but from the moment I suspected Bael was going to be with us I saw this coming.

Trick settles down on my other side and leans against me. Holding each other up, we watch the drama unfold.

"I kinda wish I had some popcorn," I say, nudging Zag's body out of my direct line of sight with my foot.

"You would say that," Trick says, smiling tiredly. "I don't

know how they have the bloody energy for it. I'm nearly comatose."

I shrug or attempt to. My shoulder moved a little, so I'm going to count it this time. "Look at it this way, they're both tired, so it shouldn't last long."

"Do you think they'll come to blows?" Why is he even asking me that?

"Well, yeah. These two have a history—not that I know what it is—I just know it exists. I'm assuming since there's animosity between them that it was bad."

"You think that one of them slept with one of their girl-friends or something?"

I snort. "No, if only it were that simple."

"So far, they haven't even managed to hit each other. All they're doing is taking turns punching air." They are, in fact circling each other like two angry tomcats. One will throw a punch, and the other moves out of the way, then rinse and repeat.

Out of habit, I give both of them the critical once over. Bael is good, really good—I'm glad he has our back, but Ciar, even as beat down as he is, is still better. I can tell by the way he's watching Bael, gauging him.

*What's the point of this?* I ask Ciar. *I thought you two buried the hatchet when we blood bonded?* I'm too tired to put much effort into stopping them. This is the natural order of things when it comes to powerful men. They always have to measure dicks.

*The pecking order must be established.*

*You sound as arrogant as he does. You sure you aren't trying to pay him back for whatever he did to piss you off eons ago?*

*Yes, I give you my word.* I believe him too.

*Then end it. I don't have any snacks, and I'm tired.*

The corner of his mouth twitches and he steps forward into Bael's personal space, spinning around, he hits him with the back of his fist, sending him flying across the clearing to hit Fluffy and bounce off.

"Now, can we stop seeing who's is bigger?" I demand out loud.

Bael has the chagrin to look a little ashamed. It doesn't make him shut his mouth, however. "It needed to happen."

"Yeah, yeah. If you wanted to know who's dick is bigger, all you had to do was ask me." Three sets of eyes bore into me. Perhaps I shouldn't have said that?

The smell of flowers fills my nose, and I smile in thankfulness as we appear in my living room. Without waiting for anyone to say anything, I climb to my feet and head straight for the kitchen. Gertie, gods bless her soul, left covered dishes on the table. Grabbing a plate full of potatoes and roast I head upstairs and stuff my face while walking.

Showering quickly, I climb into bed, shut my eyes, and as sleep tickles the edge of my consciousness try to ignore the stares that are making my neck itch.

"What?" I ask the quiet room.

"That's it?" Trick demands.

"What's it?"

"No celebration?" Groaning, I roll over and bury my face in the pillows.

"Feel free to drink yourselves stupider. I'm going to sleep."

There's a moment of silence then Bael asks, "Did she say 'stupider?'"

## CHAPTER 18

## FAERIE TOOK MY PUCA AWAY

Food cooking smells like heaven. It's the only reason I got out of bed. A bed I slept in alone. For once, I'm okay with it. I got to sleep soundly without snores and groping hands and the occasional sleepy dry hump. It happens more frequently than one would expect. I haven't had the heart to tell them that one morning, I got out of bed, and Trick was sleep humping Zag's head.

Smiling, I dig into my bowl of oatmeal, savoring the taste of cinnamon on my tongue. Before Gertie started cooking, I hated oatmeal, but she makes it taste so much better. I'm not sure if it's Brownie magic, or I've just had a lot of shitty oatmeal.

The smell of flowers makes me choke on the mouthful of food and drop my spoon on my lap. The messenger appears right as Ciar enters the kitchen. He pauses, and I see the temptation on Ciar's face to turn around and walk off before the Fairy can say anything. He fights it, but it's a close thing.

"The final Trial is one that the Lord of the Hunt must do alone." With that said, he disappears, and Ciar blows me a kiss before he too is gone. Fear runs through me like wildfire, not for myself but Ciar.

I jump to my feet and yell, "Damnit Faerie. He wasn't supposed to be alone!" I know I shouldn't curse at the goddess, but if she takes him from me I'll never worship the cow—

As I'm sucked into the colorful place, I've seen once before I know I'm in trouble.

*Do you think I'm wrong to test my son?* Her voice is everywhere and inside of me at once. This is what I get for losing my temper and control of my mouth.

My mouth chooses not to listen to that nugget of common sense as it opens and says, "Hasn't he already proven his worth to you?"

*This isn't about him proving his worth to me, child.*

"Uh, what?"

*The crown is demanding these tests. I only help him in the ways I can.*

"Isn't that the same thing?" She made the crown, so it stands to reason she controls what it does. She's talking like its a living, breathing thing.

*You love him, fiercely; this is good.*

"I'd die for him... not that I want to necessarily do that right this second."

*He's too stubborn to allow you to do that.*

Don't I know it. "That decision isn't up to him."

*Dark times are coming Fate Caller, guard your hearts well.*

Just like that, I'm back in my kitchen with oatmeal on my chin and shirt.

"Keri?" Bael questions as he walks into the kitchen. "Why do you have food all over your face?"

"Ciar has gone on the last Trial."

"Alone?" Is that concern I see on his face? Yes, yes, there's a little there.

"Yeah, he has to do this one solo."

"That's ridiculous. We're a Triad. We should be finishing out the quests with him to ensure his back is protected." He speaks so passionately that I can't help but smile.

"Aw, so are you two friends now?" He huffs and crosses his arms.

"We are no longer enemies."

"Is it because he made you fly into worm butt?"

"Has anyone ever told you how inappropriate you are at times?"

"Yeah, deal with it." I wipe my chin with the napkin Kip holds out to me from the table. Wherever I am, the little Brownie is never far away. Sometimes I want to tell him it's okay to do his own thing, but I'm not entirely sure he knows how. I imagine that living with Daya has stunted him in ways that I can't even begin to comprehend, but I can make him feel safe with us if nothing else.

"Kip, are you settling in well?" I ask, sitting back down at the table. It's either this or pacing and my legs are still sore from the fiasco of a hunt the night before.

"Oh, yes. Gertie has made me a member of her tribe. I'm so happy here," he answers, beaming at me and smoothing out the nonexistent wrinkles on his brand new shirt. Gertie is behind him with a total mom smile on her face.

"I'm so glad I met you, Gertie," I say quietly, and as she blushes I stand up and go in search of something to keep myself occupied. Sitting isn't working for me, and pacing makes Gertie itchy.

I end up hiding and pacing in front of the bedroom window that looks into Bael's old house. He's closed everything up, so the blinds are down, but thinking about the first time I stood here and what I saw temporarily distracts me.

The first time I saw Bael, creeping on me in a grocery store, I had no idea that this is where we'd end up. Two steps away from being together forever. Life works so weirdly, almost like it feels sorry for me. Taking one and replacing it with the upgraded model, well, replacing him with the one that was always meant to take his place.

It doesn't mean that part of me won't always miss Rime, just a little. I'll never forget the way he smells like a frosty cold morning and clean breezes. But I'll always remember the way he betrayed me.

"Morose thoughts so early in the morning," Trick says, coming up behind me. For a second he hesitates and then wraps his arms around my waist to rest his chin on my shoulder. I relax into his embrace. This closeness between us is still new, but I can't say I don't like it. Strangely enough for me, physical affection always makes things better.

"Feels like it happened years ago, but it was only a week, and on top of it—I feel shitty that I'm already willing to move onto someone else when he's in such pain, Trick." There's the truth of it. To say I'm taking things slow with Trick and Bael is the truth, but they will progress, Trick sooner than Bael.

Who am I kidding? Trick and I have already hit the sooner part. His arms around me belong there as much as Ciar's—thinking about him makes my heart ache even more.

"Do you think he's okay?"

"Ciar? Psh, that man can plow his way through anything. In all my years, he's the toughest bastard I've met. Damn vicious in a fight, makes me glad I'll never have to find out first hand."

"Still, I thought we were going to do them all together." Regardless of Faerie trying in her own way to reassure me—and warn me, I totally got the 'hearts' bit—its still shitty we weren't able to go with him. Who the hell makes up all these quest rules?

"I imagine some tight assholed prick who lives in a cave

alone with only pictures of his grandma to jerk off to." I give Trick a look over my shoulder. Pictures of grandma?

"Something you need to tell me?" I tease.

His cheeks redden, and he gives me a dirty look. Laughing, I twine my fingers with his and keep staring out the window. I could go to the other window and watch the street, but staring at that window and remembering is working out better for me.

The thing about emotional pain, no matter how much or little there is, it fucks with you in a way physical pain doesn't. There are ways around physical pain, but emotional pain likes to camp out in your brain and set fire to your well being. And as your burning, all of your doubt and anger feed it, making it grow bigger until it's trying to consume you. That's when you need to dump water on it. Lots of water.

Stand up to yourself and fight back. Some of the hardest battles you'll ever have to fight in life are against yourself, win as many as you can, and always keep fighting.

That's what I'm standing here doing wrapped in the arms of a man who can give me the softness I sometimes need. And in my shadow stands the man who can give me the spark, while worrying about the one who can give me more drive.

Maybe fate is kinder than I realized?

When Ciar comes home safe and in one piece, I'll truly believe it.

## CHAPTER 19
## A PRINCE TELLS ALL

Three days have passed and still no word from Ciar. He's still on the other end of the bond, but other than knowing he's there, I haven't gotten much. My agitation keeps climbing, and as mine does, so does everyone else's. The only thing keeping me from attempting to look for him is the knowledge that he's more than capable of taking care of himself. I have complete faith in that, but I won't pretend that I'm not concerned.

I love him, and I should be.

Trick has slept with me every night since Ciar's been gone, and Bael has set up a sleeping bag on the floor. If things were different, I might have invited him into the bed, but until Ciar returns home, I'm not comfortable enough to do that. It doesn't seem right to take that step without my Puca here.

Tonight is rougher, there's a thunderstorm outside, and all I can do is watch it out the window. The lightning streaking angrily across the sky is a reflection of my turbulent emotions. I'm too raw to pretend like I'm not worried. And all of the reassuring words about how tough Ciar is, aren't helpful. To me anyhow.

Ciar and I have been together for a long time. Most of my life and even the tiniest thought about living without him... let's say that I wouldn't. No way. I'm not that person who can say, 'Life moves on' yada bullshit.

More importantly, he's doing this for me, not himself. If not for this mess with Daya and the Triad, he'd have never pursued the crown. I'm not sure of everything pertaining to it anyhow. I mean, we have a High-King, how does Ciar's crown mesh with that? Does he become the king of even that king? How will Bael feel about that? Will there be more dealing with Daya? A war? That thought makes me roll over and punch the pillow where Ciar typically sleeps.

War will kill us all. Not even the guys can go up against an entire army. Faerie, I hope that's something I don't have to worry about in the future.

"He would not war with Ciar. The Fae King is revered—and until now—I thought a fictional title. Even my father has to bow to that crown, it won't give him a choice," Bael says quietly from the floor.

I look over the edge of the bed at him. He's laying on his back with his hands behind his head, staring at me. Those eyes of his are magical, and there's no other word for them. He smiles and raises an eyebrow.

"You sound pretty sure of that."

"My father is a cold bastard, but he's an honorable cold bastard. Unfortunately he's spent too much time hiding behind his walls, distant from his people. He's forgotten what it's like out here. I had too until I ran into you. I was living in a bubble created by court life and had no real concept of the outside world. You forced me to look and look deep."

"So, what will happen? You know more about this stuff than I do."

"Ciar is already recognized as a Fae Lord, and my father has long suspected that there's more to him. Wait until he finds out what it is." He chuckles, and I stare at him, waiting for the rest of the answer. "He will concede to Ciar, with the request to retain his rights as the regional king, which for Ciar would keep things less complicated. I do not doubt that Ciar can run a kingdom, but I do doubt that he wants to."

"What's your history with Ciar? No dodging or telling me to ask him, he's not exactly forthcoming about it."

"There was a woman..."

"Oh, gods... seriously?"

"Not that kind of woman. She was a healer who lived at the edge of the Dark Forgetful Forest and so old that she could barely walk to the river for water. Ciar had a soft spot for her, but the village of humans close to her did not. He came and requested permission to protect her with force if need be and father denied his request. To add to it my father told him that if he interfered he'd incarcerate him and burn down the forest."

"That's harsh, and your dad is a dick."

"He was young and new to the throne, trying to prove himself against a creature he knew to be much older and more powerful than he. That's no excuse, but it is the reason he did it."

"They killed her, didn't they?" It's awful that Ciar lost his friend that way. And makes me dislike the king even more.

"As humans often do, yes." Humans aren't all bad, but when it comes to their interactions with Fae, it's never clean cut. So much prejudice and hatred for the Fae's presence. Not that any of us had a choice.

"And you two?"

"When he came a second time, asking for help with you—I'm assuming you're the only child he took in—I taunted him for being a pussy."

"Dick."

"Yeah, I know that now, but I grew up believing that I was untouchable, and everyone else was beneath me." There's a lot of honesty in that statement, and I'm sure, in some cases still holds true, but even Ciar has witnessed the changes in him. I'm pretty sure that's the only reason Bael is here with all of his limbs still attached.

"Believing bullshit like that won't get you anywhere in life. Living with us, you'll learn that's not how the world works."

"Ciar isn't as innocent as you believe, he thwarted my father at every turn. Deliberately being a pain in the ass."

"Sounds to me like your father needs someone to keep him in check. Can't say I blame Ciar."

"I used to." That sounds promising.

"Used to?"

"Yes, used to. Life with you is an eye-opener on many fronts. I can't say it will ever be boring." He says the last bit with a smile on his face and a glint in his eyes. It's almost enough to make me roll off the bed and onto him. Almost. He's way hotter than he was in creepy stalker mode. "You thought I was creepy in the beginning?"

Oops. "Yeah, you looked at me like I was a new pet. I didn't like that look. And keep in mind I was taught that high Fae were no good for me." Most of them still aren't Bael is the exception. I still don't think I'll like his father.

"When I saw you, the world tilted on its axis. I'd never had a woman affect me in such a way before. Nor had one ever denied me." There's that arrogance that he bathes in. Even though I'm flattered I tilted his world.

"I thought you were a pretty creepy guy," I say honestly. No reason to lie and have that make yet another mess in my life.

He laughs and reaches up to touch my face. "Your honesty

is refreshing. In court, no one ever tells the full truth. I'm looking forward to turning you loose on them."

"Hey, now, no one said anything about hanging around long enough to meet anyone but your dad."

"A banquet is a gathering of all court members. There's well over a thousand of them."

"We'll be cutting that visit short."

"Ciar won't, and you know it. It'll be the perfect chance for him to formally announce his kingship. In some ways, his mind is as formal as my father's. Ciar is simply more in touch with the reality of how the world actually is. My father has convinced himself the world is how he imagines it."

"He insane?"

"No, old and set in his ways, perhaps. I think he's bored too but doesn't want to admit it."

"I'm guessing you two have a crappy relationship?"

"I'm his heir and his only child, but I was raised by nannies and my mother. He was a figure that showed up occasionally to tell me I needed to do better in something. His distance hurt more than if he'd beat my ass every day."

"Yeah, you say that not knowing what it's like to get your ass beat every day."

After staring at me, weighing my words, he says, "I concede to your point."

"If you think about it, it's rather messed up that all of us have such fucked up parents. Mine sacrificed another child to create me so that she could shape me into a murderer. Yours tried to murder you before you were born and then almost succeeded when you were a child. And Ciar's is an omnipotent goddess whose tune we dance to every day and then Bael's is a king who doesn't know how to 'people,'" Trick says in a voice muffled by a pillow.

"That's one heavy-duty summary, Trick," I say, looking at his back over my shoulder.

He chuckles and pats my butt with his hand. "Hopefully, your wily Puca can come up with a way to kick Daya's ass."

My heart rate picks up, and I know that Ciar is coming, the bond is humming with his energy, and as it culminates, he appears on the floor at the foot of the bed. He's kneeling on one knee with one hand holding him up. In the other is a shining, glorious gold crown with delicate leaves of silver woven through it.

I jump up and go to him. He's bloody and battered, half-naked. The injuries I can see on his chest and shoulders are enough to make me hesitant to touch him. He leans forward into me and shudders as I carefully wrap my arms around him.

"Will this work?" Ciar asks, his voice thick with exhaustion. He tosses the crown onto the bed and passes out in my arms.

What did they do to him?

# CHAPTER 20
## THAT'S ALMOST A WRAP

T hat's almost a wrap

IT TOOK THREE DAYS, BUT CIAR RECOVERED, HE'S BACK TO normal, mostly. There's a new potent edge to him that wasn't there before, or maybe it was, but now it's more noticeable. Since he's gotten back I refuse to stray too far from him, and so far, the Hunt hasn't called him either. Maybe Faerie is giving him a vacation after whatever he endured while he was gone? Not that he's told me anything about it.

When I woke up in the middle of the night, he was standing at the window, lost in thought. I hope that when he's ready, he'll talk to me about it. Or I'll run out of patience and push him. He's the type that needs a push sometimes to open up, and I'm the type that gets impatient. It's a flaw, but I have no plans to work on that particular one.

The crown sits on our dresser, occasionally lighting up like a low burning candle. When he looks at it, there's no satisfaction on his face, just a grim acceptance. Ciar isn't keen on being king, and as far as I know, we're the only ones who know that he is.

Bael was right about Ciar wanting to announce it at the banquet. He told me as much the first time we discussed it a couple of days ago. He smiled with satisfaction and said we'd make a big to-do over it. I don't know whether I should be nervous or anticipate whatever the mischievous Puca is planning on doing.

Not that I leave him with a lot of extra energy.

Trick and I are growing closer every day, and I'm learning things about him slowly but surely. How he was made, why he was made and what was done in order for him to be free. About broke my heart seeing that haunted look in his eyes. So I distracted him with lewd sexual acts. At some point there's a chance he was faking it just for the distractions. Either way, it works out for both of us.

Trick is a complex man in some ways, and in others he's the easiest one to read of the three. He talks for one. We have conversations about some of the most mundane things, especially what he can turn into, which is apparently, anything. Seeing a talking toilet plunger is a surreal experience, but I did get a video. There was no way I was passing on that opportunity.

Bael and Ciar talk more as equals now. I don't know if it was their pissing match or Ciar returning with the crown, but things have definitely changed between them. I don't expect them to be hugging anytime soon, but at least they're no longer enemies.

Bael is a work in progress. He's spent so much of his life being 'above' everyone that he has no idea how to wallow in the gutter with us ordinary people. Plus, watching him and Gertie argue about laundry is entertaining. He was throwing his dirty clothes away, and she was explaining the waste not, want not rule. Given that he's now putting his laundry in the basket, I think Gertie won that disagreement.

Bael is more fun than I ever thought he could be. His humor is lower key than the other two, but he does laugh with us often. A good thing for everyone. Laughter has the ability to form bonds that stick around for the long haul because then most of your memories with a person are good ones. Personally, I like making him laugh. It's deep and sexy.

The temptation it represents is hard to resist some days, but even he knows I'm not ready. Not that he's pushing me, in fact, I think he's courting me. I get flowers every day, he goes out of his way to spend time with me and slowly but surely I'm learning what kind of person is becoming part of my life.

I've accepted that our growing relationship has nothing to do with magical manipulation. We genuinely have some things in common. He even bought a ship model for us to work on together.

I'm looking forward to the day I can *work* on him too.

Zag sticks to me like glue, and when we leave the house, he's not his usual laid-back self. His head is constantly moving as he watches for any type of threat. He set a homeless man's coat on fire yesterday when he walked by on the way to the store.

And all three of the guys still try to follow me unseen. It's funny to me because they suck at it, and I'm starting to wonder if it's on purpose.

Fluffy, well, Fluffy has a home in the back field now. He's way too big to sleep in the house, so I visit him every day. Unfortunately, he doesn't shrink down like Zag, and honestly, I think he's happy out there. He dug himself a nice comfy burrow and sleeps most of the time. We're taking bets on whether or not he'll sneak and eat the Fairies' sheep. So far he's left them alone, but Fluffy likes his snacks.

Bert filed the Patron paperwork and now stops in for a visit randomly. When he stopped this morning, he and Gertie were debating on the best way to marinade Unicorn steak. I was merely curious if it had glitter in it.

It totally does.

Life has fallen into this tense normality that is getting quite boring, but I'm not going to complain. Daya is still out there, and next week, there's a king's banquet I have to attend. The good thing is that I get to buy another Fairy sewn dress. That almost makes it worth going by itself. The bad news is I have to hang around a bunch of uptight aristocrats who will look at me like I'm a turd beneath their boot.

I have no court etiquette, and I think Bael is looking forward to me upsetting that part of his world. Because they all know I will.

With a sigh, I absently chew on the chips that Gertie made me while staring out the window. When I see movement, I sit up straighter. I know that white hair.

Rime looks at me from across the street, and I know he can see me as clearly as I can see him. For several seconds I stare at him, expecting the pain to lance through my heart but it doesn't happen. Apparently, I've closed that chapter in my life for good.

When he smiles, one that reminds me so much of Daya that I get chills, and runs a finger across his throat, I almost call his fate right there. But the echo of the feelings I had for him stop me in my tracks. Something that tacky isn't a good enough reason to kill him, and I'm not even sure I can. I might not love him anymore, but I *did* love him, and that's enough to make me not want to think about it.

When he walks away, with his lips pursed like he's

whistling the foreboding feeling that tells me my hesitance will cost me settles in my stomach. Life might be quiet now, but it won't stay that way. Not until those that threaten my family and me are dealt with and now...

Rime's on that list.

# ACKNOWLEDGMENTS

*Thank you, all of you.*

## ABOUT ZOE PARKER

Zoe is an introvert who thinks people watching at Walmart is a good time. Leaving her house is rare enough that her neighbors thought she moved out. Everything in her head always ends up on paper.

I believe in Fairies, do you? Why not pick up a book and find out? (especially, if they're keen to go around shirtless.)

Www.zoeparkerbooks.com
https://www.facebook.com/ZoeParkerAuthor
https://www.facebook.com/groups/ZoesSavagesquad

ALSO BY ZOE PARKER

Facets of Feyrie Series - Urban Fantasy
Elusion, Book One
Ascension, Book Two
Deception, Book Three
Obliteration, Book Four

A Whychoose, multiple-mayhem series, The Fate Caller Series:
Cadence of Ciar, Book One
Rhythm of Rime, Book Two
Timing of Trick

Unsylum Series
Up with the Crows - Book One
As the Crow Flies - Book Two

Printed in Great Britain
by Amazon